# Nasty Endings

Dennis Pepper

*Illustrated by Martin Cottam*

OXFORD

## OTHER BOOKS BY DENNIS PEPPER

# Contents

# OXFORD
### UNIVERSITY PRESS

Great Clarendon Street, Oxford OX2 6DP

Oxford University Press is a department of the University of Oxford.
It furthers the University's objective of excellence in research, scholarship,
and education by publishing worldwide in

Oxford New York

Athens Auckland Bangkok Bogotá Buenos Aires Cape Town
Chennai Dar es Salaam Delhi Florence Hong Kong Istanbul Karachi
Kolkata Kuala Lumpur Madrid Melbourne Mexico City Mumbai
Nairobi Paris São Paulo Shanghai Singapore Taipei Tokyo Toronto Warsaw

and associated companies in Berlin Ibadan

Oxford is a registered trade mark of Oxford University Press
in the UK and in certain other countries

This selection and arrangement copyright © Dennis Pepper 1997

The moral rights of the author have been asserted

Database right Oxford University Press (maker)

These stories first published in *The Young Oxford Book of Nasty Endings* 1997,
except 'The Middle Toe of the Right Foot', 'An Alpine Divorce',
and 'The Ghost of the Blue Chamber'
First published in this paperback edition 2001

British Library Cataloguing in Publication Data available

ISBN 0 19 275143 3

1 3 5 7 9 10 8 6 4 2

Typeset by AFS Image Setters Ltd, Glasgow

Printed in Great Britain by Cox & Wyman Ltd, Reading, Berkshire

# The Landlady

### ROALD DAHL

Billy Weaver had travelled down from London on the slow afternoon train, with a change at Swindon on the way, and by the time he got to Bath it was about nine o'clock in the evening and the moon was coming up out of a clear starry sky over the houses opposite the station entrance. But the air was deadly cold and the wind was like a flat blade of ice on his cheeks.

'Excuse me,' he said, 'but is there a fairly cheap hotel not too far away from here?'

'Try The Bell and Dragon,' the porter answered, pointing down the road. 'They might take you in. It's about a quarter of a mile along on the other side.'

Billy thanked him and picked up his suitcase and set out to walk the quarter-mile to The Bell and Dragon. He had never been to Bath before. He didn't know anyone who lived there.

But Mr Greenslade at the Head Office in London had told him it was a splendid city. 'Find your own lodgings,'

1

he had said, 'and then go along and report to the Branch Manager as soon as you've got yourself settled.'

Billy was seventeen years old. He was wearing a new navy-blue overcoat, a new brown trilby hat, and a new brown suit, and he was feeling fine. He walked briskly down the street. He was trying to do everything briskly these days. Briskness, he had decided, was *the* one common characteristic of all successful businessmen. The big shots up at Head Office were absolutely fantastically brisk all the time. They were amazing.

There were no shops on this wide street that he was walking along, only a line of tall houses on each side, all of them identical. They had porches and pillars and four or five steps going up to their front doors, and it was obvious that once upon a time they had been very swanky residences. But now, even in the darkness, he could see that the paint was peeling from the woodwork on their doors and windows, and that the handsome white façades were cracked and blotchy from neglect.

Suddenly, in a downstairs window that was brilliantly illuminated by a street-lamp not six yards away, Billy caught sight of a printed notice propped up against the glass in one of the upper panes. It said BED AND BREAKFAST. There was a vase of pussy-willows, tall and beautiful, standing just underneath the notice.

He stopped walking. He moved a bit closer. Green curtains (some sort of velvety material) were hanging down on either side of the window. The pussy-willows looked wonderful beside them. He went right up and peered through the glass into the room, and the first thing he saw was a bright fire burning in the hearth. On the carpet in front of the fire, a pretty little dachshund was curled up asleep with its nose tucked into its belly.

The room itself, so far as he could see in the half-darkness, was filled with pleasant furniture. There was a baby-grand piano and a big sofa and several plump armchairs; and in one corner he spotted a large parrot in a cage. Animals were usually a good sign in a place like this, Billy told himself; and all in all, it looked to him as though it would be a pretty decent house to stay in. Certainly it would be more comfortable than The Bell and Dragon.

On the other hand, a pub would be more congenial than a boarding-house. There would be beer and darts in the evenings, and lots of people to talk to, and it would probably be a good bit cheaper, too. He had stayed a couple of nights in a pub once before and he had liked it. He had never stayed in any boarding-houses, and, to be perfectly honest, he was a tiny bit frightened of them. The name itself conjured up images of watery cabbage, rapacious landladies, and a powerful smell of kippers in the living-room.

After dithering about like this in the cold for two or three minutes, Billy decided that he would walk on and take a look at The Bell and Dragon before making up his mind. He turned to go.

And now a queer thing happened to him. He was in the act of stepping back and turning away from the window when all at once his eye was caught and held in the most peculiar manner by the small notice that was there. BED AND BREAKFAST, it said. BED AND BREAKFAST, BED AND BREAKFAST, BED AND BREAKFAST. Each word was like a large black eye staring at him through the glass, holding him, compelling him, forcing him to stay where he was and not to walk away from that house, and the next thing he knew, he was actually

3

moving across from the window to the front door of the house, climbing the steps that led up to it, and reaching for the bell.

He pressed the bell. Far away in a back room he heard it ringing, and then *at once*—it must have been at once because he hadn't even had time to take his finger from the bell-button—the door swung open and a woman was standing there.

Normally you ring the bell and you have at least a half-minute's wait before the door opens. But this dame was like a jack-in-the-box. He pressed the bell—and out she popped! It made him jump.

She was about forty-five or fifty years old, and the moment she saw him, she gave him a warm welcoming smile.

'*Please* come in,' she said pleasantly. She stepped aside, holding the door wide open, and Billy found himself automatically starting forward into the house. The compulsion or, more accurately, the desire to follow after her into that house was extraordinarily strong.

'I saw the notice in the window,' he said, holding himself back.

'Yes, I know.'

'I was wondering about a room.'

'It's *all* ready for you, my dear,' she said. She had a round pink face and very gentle blue eyes.

'I was on my way to The Bell and Dragon,' Billy told her. 'But the notice in your window just happened to catch my eye.'

'My dear boy,' she said, 'why don't you come in out of the cold?'

'How much do you charge?'

'Five and sixpence a night, including breakfast.'

It was fantastically cheap. It was less than half of what he had been willing to pay.

'If that is too much,' she added, 'then perhaps I can reduce it just a tiny bit. Do you desire an egg for breakfast? Eggs are expensive at the moment. It would he sixpence less without the egg.'

'Five and sixpence is fine,' he answered. 'I should like very much to stay here.'

'I knew you would. Do come in.'

She seemed terribly nice. She looked exactly like the mother of one's best schoolfriend welcoming one into the house to stay for the Christmas holidays. Billy took off his hat, and stepped over the threshold.

'Just hang it there,' she said, 'and let me help you with your coat.'

There were no other hats or coats in the hall. There were no umbrellas, no walking-sticks—nothing.

'We have it *all* to ourselves,' she said, smiling at him over her shoulder as she led the way upstairs. 'You see, it isn't very often I have the pleasure of taking a visitor into my little nest.'

The old girl is slightly dotty, Billy told himself. But at five and sixpence a night, who gives a damn about that? 'I should've thought you'd be simply swamped with applicants,' he said politely.

'Oh, I am, my dear, I am, of course I am. But the trouble is that I'm inclined to be just a teeny weeny bit choosy and particular—if you see what I mean.'

'Ah, yes.'

'But I'm always ready. Everything is always ready day and night in this house just on the off-chance that an acceptable young gentleman will come along. And it is such a pleasure, my dear, such a very great pleasure when now and again I open the door and I see someone standing there who is just *exactly* right.' She was half-way up the stairs, and she paused with one hand on the stair-rail, turning her head and smiling down at him with pale lips. 'Like you,' she added, and her blue eyes travelled slowly all the way down the length of Billy's body, to his feet, and then up again.

On the first-floor landing she said to him, 'This floor is mine.'

They climbed up a second flight. 'And this one is *all* yours,' she said. 'Here's your room. I do hope you'll like it.' She took him into a small but charming front bedroom, switching on the light as she went in.

'The morning sun comes right in the window, Mr Perkins. It *is* Mr Perkins, isn't it?'

'No,' he said. 'It's Weaver.'

'Mr Weaver. How nice. I've put a water-bottle between the sheets to air them out, Mr Weaver. It's such a comfort to have a hot water-bottle in a strange bed with clean sheets, don't you agree? And you may light the gas fire at any time if you feel chilly.'

'Thank you,' Billy said. 'Thank you ever so much.' He noticed that the bedspread had been taken off the bed, and that the bedclothes had been neatly turned back on one side, all ready for someone to get in.

'I'm so glad you appeared,' she said, looking earnestly into his face. 'I was beginning to get worried.'

'That's all right,' Billy answered brightly. 'You mustn't worry about me.' He put his suitcase on the chair and started to open it.

'And what about supper, my dear? Did you manage to get anything to eat before you came here?'

'I'm not a bit hungry, thank you,' he said. 'I think I'll

just go to bed as soon as possible because tomorrow I've
got to get up rather early and report to the office.'

'Very well, then. I'll leave you now so that you can
unpack. But before you go to bed, would you be kind
enough to pop into the sitting-room on the ground floor
and sign the book? Everyone has to do that because it's
the law of the land, and we don't want to go breaking any
laws at *this* stage in the proceedings, do we?' She gave
him a little wave of the hand and went quickly out of the
room and closed the door.

Now, the fact that his landlady appeared to be slightly
off her rocker didn't worry Billy in the least. After all, she
was not only harmless—there was no question about
that—but she was also quite obviously a kind and
generous soul. He guessed that she had probably lost a
son in the war, or something like that, and had never got
over it.

So a few minutes later, after unpacking his suitcase
and washing his hands, he trotted downstairs to the
ground floor and entered the living-room. His landlady
wasn't there, but the fire was glowing in the hearth, and
the little dachshund was still sleeping in front of it. The
room was wonderfully warm and cosy. I'm a lucky fellow,
he thought, rubbing his hands. This is a bit of all right.

He found the guest-book lying open on the piano, so
he took out his pen and wrote down his name and
address. There were only two other entries above his on
the page, and, as one always does with guest-books, he
started to read them. One was a Christopher Mulholland
from Cardiff. The other was Gregory W. Temple from
Bristol.

That's funny, he thought suddenly. Christopher
Mulholland. It rings a bell.

Now where on earth had he heard that rather unusual name before?

Was he a boy at school? No. Was it one of his sister's numerous young men, perhaps, or a friend of his father's? No, no, it wasn't any of those. He glanced down again at the book.

*Christopher Mulholland    231 Cathedral Road, Cardiff*
*Gregory W. Temple         27 Sycamore Drive, Bristol*

As a matter of fact, now he came to think of it, he wasn't at all sure that the second name didn't have almost as much of a familiar ring about it as the first.

'Gregory Temple?' he said aloud, searching his memory. 'Christopher Mulholland? . . . '

'Such charming boys,' a voice behind him answered, and he turned and saw his landlady sailing into the room with a large silver tea-tray in her hands. She was holding it well out in front of her, and rather high up, as though the tray were a pair of reins on a frisky horse.

'They sound somehow familiar,' he said.

'They do? How interesting.'

'I'm almost positive I've heard those names before somewhere. Isn't that queer? Maybe it was in the newspapers. They weren't famous in any way, were they? I mean famous cricketers or footballers or something like that?'

'Famous,' she said, setting the tea-tray down on the low table in front of the sofa. 'Oh no, I don't think they were famous. But they were extraordinarily handsome, both of them, I can promise you that. They were tall and young and handsome, my dear, just exactly like you.'

Once more, Billy glanced down at the book. 'Look

here,' he said, noticing the dates. 'This last entry is over two years old.'

'It is?'

'Yes, indeed. And Christopher Mulholland's is nearly a year before that—more than *three years* ago.'

'Dear me,' she said, shaking her head and heaving a dainty little sigh. 'I would never have thought it. How time does fly away from us all, doesn't it, Mr Wilkins?'

'It's Weaver,' Billy said. 'W-e-a-v-e-r.'

'Oh, of course it is!' she cried, sitting down on the sofa. 'How silly of me. I do apologize. In one ear and out the other, that's me, Mr Weaver.'

'You know something?' Billy said. 'Something that's really quite extraordinary about all this?'

'No, dear, I don't.'

'Well, you see—both of these names, Mulholland and Temple, I not only seem to remember each one of them separately, so to speak, but somehow or other, in some peculiar way, they both appear to be sort of connected together as well. As though they were both famous for the same sort of thing, if you see what I mean—like . . . well . . . like Dempsey and Tunney, for example, or Churchill and Roosevelt.'

'How amusing,' she said. 'But come over here now, dear, and sit down beside me on the sofa and I'll give you a nice cup of tea and a ginger biscuit before you go to bed.'

'You really shouldn't bother,' Billy said. 'I didn't mean you to do anything like that.' He stood by the piano, watching her as she fussed about with the cups and saucers. He noticed that she had small, white, quickly moving hands, and red finger-nails.

'I'm almost positive it was in the newspapers I saw

9

them,' Billy said. 'I'll think of it in a second. I'm sure I will.'

There is nothing more tantalizing than a thing like this which lingers just outside the borders of one's memory. He hated to give up.

'Now wait a minute,' he said. 'Wait just a minute. Mulholland . . . Christopher Mulholland . . . wasn't *that* the name of the Eton schoolboy who was on a walking-tour through the West Country, and then all of a sudden—'

'Milk?' she said. 'And sugar?'

'Yes, please. And then all of a sudden—'

'Eton schoolboy?' she said. 'Oh no, my dear, that can't possibly be right because *my* Mr Mulholland was certainly not an Eton schoolboy when he came to me. He was a Cambridge undergraduate. Come over here now and sit next to me and warm yourself in front of this lovely fire. Come on. Your tea's all ready for you.' She patted the empty place beside her on the sofa, and she sat there smiling at Billy and waiting for him to come over.

He crossed the room slowly, and sat down on the edge of the sofa. She placed his teacup on the table in front of him.

'*There* we are,' she said. 'How nice and cosy this is, isn't it?'

Billy started sipping his tea. She did the same. For half a minute or so, neither of them spoke. But Billy knew that she was looking at him. Her body was half-turned towards him, and he could feel her eyes resting on his face, watching him over the rim of her teacup. Now and again, he caught a whiff of a peculiar smell that seemed to emanate directly from her person. It was not in the least unpleasant, and it reminded him—well, he wasn't quite sure what it reminded him of. Pickled walnuts? New leather? Or was it the corridors of a hospital?

'Mr Mulholland was a great one for his tea,' she said at length. 'Never in my life have I seen anyone drink as much tea as dear, sweet Mr Mulholland.'

'I suppose he left fairly recently,' Billy said. He was still puzzling his head about the two names. He was positive now that he had seen them in the newspapers— in the headlines.

'Left?' she said, arching her brows. 'But, my dear boy, he never left. He's still here. Mr Temple is also here. They're on the third floor, both of them together.'

Billy set down his cup slowly on the table, and stared at his landlady. She smiled back at him, and then she put out one of her white hands and patted him comfortingly on the knee. 'How old are you, my dear?' she asked.

'Seventeen.'

'Seventeen!' she cried. 'Oh, it's the perfect age! Mr Mulholland was also seventeen. But I think he was a trifle shorter than you are, in fact I'm sure he was, and his teeth weren't *quite* so white. You have the most beautiful teeth, Mr Weaver, did you know that?'

'They're not as good as they look,' Billy said. 'They've got simply masses of fillings in them at the back.'

'Mr Temple, of course, was a little older,' she said, ignoring his remark. 'He was actually twenty-eight. And yet I never would have guessed it if he hadn't told me, never in my whole life. There wasn't a *blemish* on his body.'

'A what?' Billy said.

'His skin was *just* like a baby's.'

There was a pause. Billy picked up his teacup and took another sip of his tea, then he set it down again gently in its saucer. He waited for her to say something else, but she seemed to have lapsed into another of her silences. He sat there staring straight ahead of him into the far corner of the room, biting his lower lip.

'That parrot,' he said at last. 'You know something? It had me completely fooled when I first saw it through the window from the street. I could have sworn it was alive.'

'Alas, no longer.'

'It's most terribly clever the way it's been done,' he said. 'It doesn't look in the least bit dead. Who did it?'

'I did.'

'*You* did?'

'Of course,' she said. 'And have you met my little Basil as well?' She nodded towards the dachshund curled up so comfortably in front of the fire. Billy looked at it. And suddenly, he realized that this animal had all the time been just as silent and motionless as the parrot. He put out a hand and touched it gently on the top of its back. The back was hard and cold, and when he pushed the hair to one side with his fingers, he could see the skin underneath, greyish-black and dry and perfectly preserved.

'Good gracious me,' he said. 'How absolutely fascinating.' He turned away from the dog and stared with deep admiration at the little woman beside him on the sofa. 'It must be most awfully difficult to do a thing like that.'

'Not in the least,' she said. 'I stuff *all* my little pets myself when they pass away. Will you have another cup of tea?'

'No, thank you,' Billy said. The tea tasted faintly of bitter almonds, and he didn't much care for it.

'You did sign the book, didn't you?'

'Oh, yes.'

'That's good. Because later on, if I happen to forget what you were called, then I can always come down here and look it up. I still do that almost every day with Mr Mulholland and Mr . . . Mr . . . '

'Temple,' Billy said. 'Gregory Temple. Excuse my asking, but haven't there been *any* other guests here except them in the last two or three years?'

Holding her teacup high in one hand, inclining her head slightly to the left, she looked up at him out of the corners of her eyes and gave him another gentle little smile.

'No, my dear,' she said. 'Only you.'

# Revival Meeting

### DANNIE PLACHTA

Graham Kraken lay upon his deathbed. His eyes wavering upon a dim and far-away ceiling, he savoured the reassuring words.

'The odds are all in your favour,' the doctor said.

The bed seemed to tense beneath Kraken. Springs coiled tautly.

'Some day—' the doctor's voice rang with tiny, metallic chimes—'medical science will have advanced far enough to revive you. Your frozen body will not deteriorate in the interim.' The chimes grew hushed. 'Some day science will repair your body and you will live again.'

Graham Kraken died easily and they froze his corpse.

He dreamed that he was in Miami Beach and opened his eyes. Blinking into the dimness of his room, he found a visitor seated at his bedside.

'Good morning,' said the visitor.

The stranger, Kraken noted, was an elderly gentleman with a bald head and a pleasant face.

'Good morning,' said Kraken in a friendly manner. 'Nice ear-rings you have there.'

'Thank you,' said the visitor. 'They're antennae.'

'Oh?'

'For the transistor radios built into my earlobes.'

'Indeed?'

'Stereo.'

'How nice,' said Kraken. 'How do you turn it off?'

'Don't,' the visitor responded. 'Speak up a bit, please.'

'I'm sorry,' said Kraken. 'I didn't know.'

'Nice weather we're having.'

'I hadn't really noticed. By the way, have they done anything about that?'

'Well, they did for a short time,' the old gentleman said. 'But they had to give it up.'

'Too many conflicting wishes?'

'I'm afraid so.'

'A pity.' Kraken glanced at the heavily curtained window. As he watched, the glass behind the curtains suddenly shattered. 'Oh?' he said. 'Riots?'

'No,' replied the visitor. 'Supersonic transports.'

Another pane of glass automatically slipped into place.

'I guess you get quite a lot of that.'

'Easy come, easy go.'

'By the way,' Graham Kraken asked, 'what year is this?'

'Twenty-eighty-eight,' he said.

'Well,' said Kraken, 'it has been a while.'

'One year is pretty much like another,' said the stranger.

'How about the money?' wondered Kraken. 'Did my estate hold out?'

'I'm afraid not,' said the visitor. 'I had to pay for your revival.'

'That was very kind of you,' said Kraken. He noticed the sunlight edging the window curtains.

He rose upon an elbow. The motion made him feel faint.

'Please don't try to move,' the visitor said. 'It's important that you rest for the heart transplant.'

'Oh?' Kraken leaned back. 'Is there something wrong with my heart?'

The visitor stood up slowly.

'No,' he replied, 'but there's something wrong with mine.'

# The Middle Toe of the Right Foot

## AMBROSE BIERCE

It is well known that the old Manton house is haunted. In all the rural district near about, and even in the town of Marshall, a mile away, not one person of unbiased mind entertains a doubt of it; incredulity is confined to those opinionated persons who will be called 'cranks' as soon as the useful word shall have penetrated the intellectual demesne of the Marshall *Advance*. The evidence that the house is haunted is of two kinds: the testimony of disinterested witnesses who have had ocular proof, and that of the house itself. The former may be disregarded and ruled out on any of the various grounds of objection which may be urged against it by the ingenious; but facts within the observation of all are material and controlling.

In the first place, the Manton house has been unoccupied by mortals for more than ten years, and with its outbuildings is slowly falling into decay—a circumstance which in itself the judicious will hardly venture to ignore. It stands a little way off the loneliest reach of the Marshall and Harriston road, in an opening which was once a farm and is still disfigured with strips of rotting fence and half covered with brambles overrunning a stony and sterile soil long unacquainted with the plough. The house itself is in tolerably good condition, though badly weather-stained and in dire need of attention from the glazier, the smaller male population of the region having attested in the manner of its kind its disapproval of dwelling without dwellers. It is two storeys in height, nearly square, its front pierced by a single doorway flanked on each side by a window boarded up to the very top. Corresponding windows above, not protected, serve to admit light and rain to the rooms of the upper floor. Grass and weeds grow pretty rankly all about, and a few shade trees, somewhat the worse for wind, and leaning all in one direction, seem to be making a concerted effort to run away. In short, as the Marshall town humourist explained in the columns of the *Advance*, 'the proposition that the Manton house is badly haunted is the only logical conclusion from the premises.' The fact that in this dwelling Mr Manton thought it expedient one night some ten years ago to rise and cut the throats of his wife and two small children, removing at once to another part of the country, has no doubt done its share in directing public attention to the fitness of the place for supernatural phenomena.

To this house, one summer evening, came four men in a wagon. Three of them promptly alighted, and the one who had been driving hitched the team to the only remaining post of what had been a fence. The fourth remained seated in the wagon. 'Come,' said one of his companions, approaching him, while the others moved away in the direction of the dwelling—'this is the place.'

The man addressed did not move. 'By God!' he said harshly, 'this is a trick, and it looks to me as if you were in it.'

'Perhaps I am,' the other said, looking him straight in the face and speaking in a tone which had something of contempt in it. 'You will remember, however, that the choice of place was with your own assent left to the other side. Of course if you are afraid of spooks—'

'I am afraid of nothing,' the man interrupted with another oath, and sprang to the ground. The two then joined the others at the door, which one of them had already opened with some difficulty, caused by rust of lock and hinge. All entered. Inside it was dark, but the man who had unlocked the door produced a candle and matches and made a light. He then unlocked a door on their right as they stood in the passage. This gave them entrance to a large, square room that the candle but dimly lighted. The floor had a thick carpeting of dust, which partly muffled their footfalls. Cobwebs were in the angles of the walls and depended from the ceiling like strips of rotting lace, making undulatory movements in the disturbed air. The room had two windows in adjoining sides, but from neither could anything be seen except the rough inner surfaces of boards a few inches from the glass. There was no fireplace, no furniture; there was nothing: besides the cobwebs and the dust, the four men were the only objects there which were not a part of the structure.

Strange enough they looked in the yellow light of the candle. The one who had so reluctantly alighted was especially spectacular—he might have been called sensational. He was of middle age, heavily built, deep chested and broad shouldered. Looking at his figure, one would have said that he had a giant's strength; at his features, that he would use it like a giant. He was clean shaven, his hair rather closely cropped and grey. His low forehead was seamed with wrinkles above the eyes, and over the nose these became vertical. The heavy black brows followed the same law, saved from meeting only by an upward turn at what would otherwise have been the point of contact. Deeply sunken beneath these, glowed in the obscure light a pair of eyes of uncertain colour, but obviously enough too small. There was something forbidding in their expression, which was not bettered by the cruel mouth and wide jaw. The nose was well enough, as noses go; one does not expect much of noses. All that was sinister in the man's face seemed accentuated by an unnatural pallor—he appeared altogether bloodless.

The appearance of the other men was sufficiently commonplace: they were such persons as one meets and forgets that he met. All were younger than the man described, between whom and the eldest of the others, who stood apart, there was apparently no kindly feeling. They avoided looking at each other.

'Gentlemen,' said the man holding the candle and keys, 'I believe everything is right. Are you ready, Mr Rosser?'

The man standing apart from the group bowed and smiled.

'And you, Mr Grossmith?'

The heavy man bowed and scowled.

'You will be pleased to remove your outer clothing.'

Their hats, coats, waistcoats, and neckwear were soon removed and thrown outside the door, in the passage. The man with the candle now nodded, and the fourth man—

he who had urged Grossmith to leave the wagon—
produced from the pocket of his overcoat two long,
murderous-looking bowie-knives, which he drew now
from their leather scabbards.

'They are exactly alike,' he said, presenting one to each
of the two principals—for by this time the dullest observer
would have understood the nature of this meeting. It was
to be a duel to the death.

Each combatant took a knife, examined it critically
near the candle and tested the strength of blade and
handle across his lifted knee. Their persons were then
searched in turn, each by the second of the other.

'If it is agreeable to you, Mr Grossmith,' said the man
holding the light, 'you will place yourself in that corner.'

He indicated the angle of the room furthest from the
door, whither Grossmith retired, his second parting from
him with a grasp of the hand which had nothing of
cordiality in it. In the angle nearest the door Mr Rosser
stationed himself, and after a whispered consultation his
second left him, joining the other near the door. At that
moment the candle was suddenly extinguished, leaving
all in profound darkness. This may have been done by a
draught from the opened door; whatever the cause, the
effect was startling.

'Gentlemen,' said a voice which sounded strangely
unfamiliar in the altered condition affecting the relations
of the senses—'gentlemen, you will not move until you
hear the closing of the outer door.'

A sound of trampling ensued, then the closing of the
inner door; and finally the outer one closed with a
concussion which shook the entire building.

A few minutes afterwards a belated farmer's boy met
a light wagon which was being driven furiously toward

the town of Marshall. He declared that behind the two figures on the front seat stood a third, with its hands upon the bowed shoulders of the others, who appeared to struggle vainly to free themselves from its grasp. This figure, unlike the others, was clad in white, and had undoubtedly boarded the wagon as it passed the haunted house. As the lad could boast a considerable former experience with the supernatural thereabouts his word had the weight justly due to the testimony of an expert. The story (in connection with the next day's events) eventually appeared in the *Advance*, with some slight literary embellishments and a concluding intimation that the gentlemen referred to would be allowed the use of the paper's columns for their version of the night's adventure. But the privilege remained without a claimant.

The events that led up to this 'duel in the dark' were simple enough. One evening three young men of the town of Marshall were sitting in a quiet corner of the porch of the village hotel, smoking and discussing such matters as three educated young men of a Southern village would naturally find interesting. Their names were King, Sancher, and Rosser. At a little distance, within easy hearing, but taking no part in the conversation, sat a fourth. He was a stranger to the others. They merely knew that on his arrival by the stagecoach that afternoon he had written in the hotel register the name Robert Grossmith. He had not been observed to speak to anyone except the hotel clerk. He seemed, indeed, singularly fond of his own company—or, as the *personnel* of the *Advance* expressed it, 'grossly addicted to evil associations.' But then it should be said in justice to the stranger that the *personnel* was himself of a too convivial disposition fairly to judge one differently gifted, and had, moreover, experienced a slight rebuff in an effort at an 'interview'.

'I hate any kind of deformity in a woman,' said King, 'whether natural or—acquired. I have a theory that any physical defect has its correlative mental and moral defect.'

'I infer, then,' said Rosser, gravely, 'that a lady lacking the moral advantage of a nose would find the struggle to become Mrs King an arduous enterprise.'

'Of course you may put it that way,' was the reply; 'but, seriously, I once threw over a most charming girl on learning quite accidentally that she had suffered amputation of a toe. My conduct was brutal if you like, but if I had married that girl I should have been miserable for life and should have made her so.'

'Whereas,' said Sancher, with a light laugh, 'by marrying a gentleman of more liberal views she escaped with a parted throat.'

'Ah, you know to whom I refer. Yes, she married Manton, but I don't know about his liberality; I'm not sure but he cut her throat because he discovered that she lacked that excellent thing in woman, the middle toe of the right foot.'

'Look at that chap!' said Rosser in a low voice, his eyes fixed upon the stranger.

That chap was obviously listening intently to the conversation.

'Damn his impudence!' muttered King—'what ought we to do?'

'That's an easy one,' Rosser replied, rising. 'Sir,' he continued, addressing the stranger, 'I think it would be better if you would remove your chair to the other end of the veranda. The presence of gentlemen is evidently an unfamiliar situation to you.'

The man sprang to his feet and strode forward with clenched hands, his face white with rage. All were now standing. Sancher stepped between the belligerents.

'You are hasty and unjust,' he said to Rosser; 'this gentleman has done nothing to deserve such language.'

But Rosser would not withdraw a word. By the custom of the country and the time there could be but one outcome to the quarrel.

'I demand the satisfaction due to a gentleman,' said the stranger, who had become more calm. 'I have not an acquaintance in this region. Perhaps you, sir,' bowing to Sancher, 'will be kind enough to represent me in this matter.'

Sancher accepted the trust—somewhat reluctantly it must be confessed, for the man's appearance and manner were not at all to his liking. King, who during the colloquy had hardly removed his eyes from the stranger's face and had not spoken a word, consented with a nod to act for Rosser, and the upshot of it was that, the principals having retired, a meeting was arranged for the next evening. The nature of the arrangements has been already disclosed. The duel with knives in a dark room was once a commoner feature of South-western life than it is likely to be again. How thin a veneering of 'chivalry' covered the essential brutality of the code under which such encounters were possible we shall see.

In the blaze of a midsummer noonday the old Manton house was hardly true to its traditions. It was of the earth, earthy. The sunshine caressed it warmly and affectionately, with evident disregard of its bad reputation.

The grass greening all the expanse in its front seemed to grow, not rankly, but with a natural and joyous exuberance, and the weeds blossomed quite like plants. Full of charming lights and shadows and populous with pleasant-voiced birds, the neglected shade trees no longer struggled to run away, but bent reverently beneath their burdens of sun and song. Even in the glassless upper windows was an expression of peace and contentment, due to the light within. Over the stony fields the visible heat danced with a lively tremor incompatible with the gravity which is an attribute of the supernatural.

Such was the aspect under which the place presented itself to Sheriff Adams and two other men who had come out from Marshall to look at it. One of these men was Mr King, the sheriff's deputy; the other, whose name was Brewer, was a brother of the late Mrs Manton. Under a beneficent law of the State relating to property which has been for a certain period abandoned by an owner whose residence cannot be ascertained, the sheriff was legal custodian of the Manton farm and appurtenances thereunto belonging. His present visit was in mere perfunctory compliance with some order of a court in which Mr Brewer had an action to get possession of the property as heir to his deceased sister. By a mere coincidence, the visit was made on the day after the night that Deputy King had unlocked the house for another and very different purpose. His presence now was not of his own choosing: he had been ordered to accompany his superior and at the moment could think of nothing more prudent than simulated alacrity in obedience to the command.

Carelessly opening the front door, which to his surprise was not locked, the sheriff was amazed to see, lying on the floor of the passage into which it opened, a confused heap of men's apparel. Examination showed it to consist of two hats, and the same number of coats, waistcoats, and scarves, all in a remarkably good state of preservation, albeit somewhat defiled by the dust in which they lay. Mr Brewer was equally astonished, but Mr King's emotion is not of record. With a new and lively interest in his own actions the sheriff now unlatched and pushed open a door on the right, and the three entered. The room was apparently vacant—no; as their eyes became accustomed to the dimmer light something was visible in the furthest angle of the wall. It was a human figure—that of a man crouching close in the corner. Something in the attitude made the intruders halt when they had barely passed the threshold. The figure more and more clearly defined itself. The man was upon one knee, his back in the angle of the wall, his shoulders elevated to the level of his ears, his hands before his face, palms outward, the fingers spread and crooked like claws; the white face turned upwards on the retracted neck had an expression of unutterable fright, the mouth half open, the eyes incredibly expanded. He was stone dead. Yet, with the exception of a bowie-knife, which had evidently fallen from his own hand, not another object was in the room.

In thick dust that covered the floor were some confused footprints near the door and along the wall through which it opened. Along one of the adjoining walls, too, past the boarded-up windows, was the trail made by the man himself in reaching his corner. Instinctively in approaching the body the three men followed that trail. The sheriff grasped one of the out-thrown arms; it was as rigid as iron, and the application of a gentle force rocked the entire body without altering the relation of its parts.

Brewer, pale with excitement, gazed intently into the distorted face. 'God of mercy!' he suddenly cried, 'it is Manton!'

'You are right,' said King, with an evident attempt at calmness: 'I knew Manton. He then wore a full beard and his hair long, but this is he.'

He might have added: 'I recognized him when he challenged Rosser. I told Rosser and Sancher who he was before we played him this horrible trick. When Rosser left this dark room at our heels, forgetting his outer clothing in the excitement, and driving away with us in his shirt sleeves—all through the discreditable proceedings we knew whom we were dealing with, murderer and coward that he was!'

But nothing of this did Mr King say. With his better light he was trying to penetrate the mystery of the man's death. That he had not once moved from the corner where he had been stationed; that his posture was that of neither attack nor defence; that he had dropped his weapon; that he had obviously perished of sheer horror of something that he *saw*—these were circumstances which Mr King's disturbed intelligence could not rightly comprehend.

Groping in intellectual darkness for a clue to his maze of doubt, his gaze, directed mechanically downwards in the way of one who ponders momentous matters, fell upon something which, there, in the light of day and in the presence of living companions, affected him with terror. In the dust of years that lay thick upon the floor— leading from the door by which they had entered, straight across the room to within a yard of Manton's crouching corpse—were three parallel lines of footprints—light but definite impressions of bare feet, the outer ones those of small children, the inner a woman's. From the point at

27

which they ended they did not return; they pointed all one way. Brewer, who had observed them at the same moment, was leaning forwards in an attitude of rapt attention, horribly pale.

'Look at that!' he cried, pointing with both hands at the nearest print of the woman's right foot, where she had apparently stopped and stood. 'The middle toe is missing—it was Gertrude!'

Gertrude was the late Mrs Manton, sister to Mr Brewer.

# Sweet Shop

### MARC ALEXANDER

To the girl it seemed an age since the day her troubles had begun—Black Monday she called it—but in fact it was only the week before. On that afternoon she sat in Eng. Lit. class fiddling with her hair ribbon, which she always did when she was bored, while Mr South rambled on about tales, of all things.

'There's a lot more to traditional fairy stories than you ever imagined when your teacher read ''Jack and the Beanstalk'' to you in the Infants,' he said, his specs flashing as they always did when he tried to get the class interested in his subject. 'What people thought of as magic in them was really glimpses of the future . . .'

'Do you believe in fairies, sir?' asked Hughie Cooper in a voice so respectful that some of the class could not help giggling.

'Oh yes, he does!' someone called out as they do in the panto.

'Oh no, he don't!' the class chorused, and this went on for a while. When it was quiet again Mr South said,

'Think of what I was saying—in the story of Snow White there was a magic mirror. What would that be today?'

'The telly, sir,' the class answered.

'And Seven-League Boots?'

Everyone shouted something different, and in the end Mr South agreed with those who said motor cars.

'And the Magic Carpet?'

'Please, sir,' said Hughie Cooper, 'isn't the Magic Carpet in *The Arabian Nights*, sir? Not in fairy tales, sir?'

Mr South pretended not to hear, and beamed when Betty Reynolds said, 'Concorde, sir?'

'What about ''Puss in Boots'', sir?' a boy asked from the back.

'That's a moggy in a chemist's shop,' said Hughie and there was a gale of laughter.

Mr South was getting angry but the buzzer saved the situation. It was home time and laughs were over for the day.

'Now think about fairy stories,' he shouted over the banging of desk tops. 'Next lesson you will write me an essay on fairy-tale things in modern life . . . '

In the playground the girl met her brother—being a year older than her he was in another class—and they walked home together. She told him about Mr South and his soppy fairy tales and he told her how someone had worked out a new video game in computer studies, and before long they were in their street which ran down to the canal.

'Hey, there's Dad's bike against the fence,' the boy said. 'Wonder why he's home?'

Even as he spoke the girl felt scared—she just knew that something was wrong, and as soon as they went inside she found out what it was. Their father was sitting at the kitchen table with a funny-not-ha-ha look on his face and a mug of tea in front of him.

'Your dad's been made redundant!' shouted Dora, their father's second wife. They could not bring themselves to call her 'mother'.

'Twenty-five years I've been at Holroyd's,' he said slowly. 'And even if I say so myself I was their best joiner in the hand-made furniture shop—and now I've been chucked out like an old boot. Seems there's no call for hand-made furniture any more, so the whole shop's being closed. They'll carry on making mass-produced rubbish— probably with robots!—but they don't need craftsmen any more. And in my day it took a five years' apprenticeship to learn the skills . . . '

'Pity you hadn't learned something more useful,' Dora said with her special sniff.

'Like what?' her husband demanded.

'Like being a clerk with the Council or a traffic warden—you don't hear of them being made redundant.'

'But I'm a joiner. Whatever ability God gave me is in my hands.'

Dora sniffed again and dabbed her eyes with the tea towel.

'Don't take on, love,' he said. 'I'll get something else.'

'You've no chance,' she replied angrily. 'Half the factories in this town are closed, so who do you think would want you at your age!'

'You can't blame me for the recession! I did think I might find some sympathy in my own home.'

'So it's sympathy you want! But what about me? Did you think about me when you let them sack you? How am I going to manage, answer me that—with those two not bringing in a penny and eating their heads off? . . . It's about time they made their own way in the world.'

'Dora, they're only school kids.'

'They cost as much as adults to keep. With you on the Unemployment I don't know what will happen.'

Their father stood up and said in a shaky voice, 'Well, I'll be off down to the Job Centre.' And he walked out.

The children exchanged a look and went outside but their father was already striding quickly down the long street.

'We'd better not go after him,' the girl said. 'He'll want to be alone for a bit.'

'Why the hell did he have to marry again?' demanded her brother.

'I suppose he was lonely.'

'He's got all the company he needs now. She could have laid off him on a day like this.'

Suddenly the girl laughed, a bitter, unsteady laugh. 'Now I know what old South was on about with his talk of fairy tales in the present day,' she said. 'There *are* still such things as witches!'

The boy looked bewildered so she said, 'Forget it—let's go down to the canal.'

When she was a little girl the canal bank had been her favourite place. In those days working boats tied up by the factories which backed on to the canal, but now a lot of them were empty and the boats did not come any more. The water was stagnant and people threw rubbish into it, but it was still peaceful. As the two children strolled along the old towpath they saw a silent angler with a fishing rod hoping to land a tiddler which had survived the pollution.

'As soon as I can I'm going away,' said the boy. Then he added, 'You can come with me, if you like.'

'Thanks.'

'I'm sick of it all—Dora's nagging, and the endless rows. We used to have such a good time. Seems like ages ago now.'

His sister took his hand but could think of nothing to say.

The canal ran through the town but as it was hidden away behind buildings most people had forgotten about it, which made it a secret way for the children to wander until they found they were in a part of the town which was strange to them.

'This must be the Old Town where the Council was going to build those new blocks of flats,' said the boy. 'Let's go and see what it's like.'

They went up a narrow passage between two warehouses and found themselves in a street where most of the houses had been knocked down. This had been done to make way for tower blocks but the Council had run out of money and the place looked like an old battlefield. Here and there a few houses, some lonely shops and a boarded-up church survived among the rubble. At the end of the street a building stood by itself and as the children drew nearer they gave whistles of surprise—it was a sweet shop. Its paint was bright, its glass shone in the sunlight, and it had a sign on which GINGERBREAD was painted in large golden letters.

They went up to the window and there was another surprise—it was crammed with the biggest assortment of sweets they had ever seen. The display was not made up of Mars bars and such-like but old-fashioned lollies in big glass jars, sweets that their mother—their real mother— told them she used to get when she was a girl, and which had to be weighed and put in little white paper bags.

'It can't do much business here,' said the boy. 'But look at those jelly babies . . . '

'There's a jar of aniseed balls . . . '

'Gob stoppers . . . '

'Chocolate fish . . . '

'If you're so interested, why not come inside,' said a soft voice, and they saw a plump white-haired old lady smiling at them from the door. The only odd thing about her was her spectacles, which magnified her eyes to twice their normal size, but the children soon got used to her appearance.

Inside the shop she gave them different sweets to try until the boy, feeling he should spend some money, bought a quarter of Pontefract cakes.

'Look, I have some gingerbread men,' said the old lady. 'Do you know the story of the Gingerbread Man?'

'My mum told me when I was small, and I cried at the way the Gingerbread Man kept losing pieces of himself as he ran away,' the girl said. 'It seemed so sad.'

'But not for those who were eating him,' chuckled the old lady. She was pleased to have someone to talk to because, as she told them, she had lost most of her customers when the houses were demolished but she loved her shop and did not want to leave it. They stayed chatting with her until it was twilight outside, and they had forgotten what had happened at home.

'Come back to Gingerbread any time,' she said as they left. 'My name is Hazel—the kiddies used to call me Aunt Hazel. You can if you like.'

When they got back to the towpath the girl found that the old lady had slipped a big bar of fruit-and-nut into her pocket.

'What a nice old dear,' she said as she shared it with her brother.

'Her shop reminds me of a picture I once saw in a storybook,' he said. 'I didn't think there were any shops like that left.'

'It's a find. Perhaps I will come back and see her.'

'You're just out for free chocolate,' he teased.


Next morning the two children did not wait to have breakfast but hurried out. They were sick of the quarrelling that had flared up the night before, when Dora had accused them of always plotting against her because she had the bad luck to be their stepmother. It was something that had not occurred to her until their father had been made redundant.

When they reached the corner the boy said, 'I'm going to cut school today.'

The girl nodded.

'Let's go for a walk.'

'Poor Dad, all those years at Holroyd's . . . and Dora going on as though it's his fault.'

Without either of them discussing where they were going, they arrived at the cemetery. In front of the gravestone with their mother's name on it was a bunch of carnations, and they realized that it was not to the Job Centre that their father had gone the night before.

Later they found themselves wandering along the canal bank, a place where they were less likely to be reported for playing truant.

'I know,' said the boy suddenly. 'Let's go and see Aunt Hazel—you might get given another bar of chocolate.'

They arrived at the shop called Gingerbread and had

just enough money to buy a quarter of old-fashioned cough candy.

'You're not at school?' said Aunt Hazel, staring at them with her magnified eyes.

'We gave ourselves a holiday,' the girl said, and she laughed.

'I'm glad. I was feeling lonely. Sometimes I don't open the shop in the mornings because no one comes—my only customers are kids from the Council estate over there, and they come after school. But I'm glad I opened up today because you both look as though you have troubles.'

'We're all right,' said the boy quickly.

'Good, but as you are on holiday you can at least have a cup of tea with me.'

Having missed breakfast they were happy to follow her into her living-room which was just as quaint as the shop, and full of old-fashioned furniture which would have delighted their father. In front of an open fireplace dozed one of the biggest black cats they had ever seen, and there was a parrot in a big cage who chattered, 'Open the door—let me out.'

Aunt Hazel tapped the cage and said, 'Silly thing, you know Samkin would have your tailfeathers the moment you were outside.' But the parrot kept on saying 'Let me out' until she put a cloth over his cage and he thought it was night time.

'Why do you have bars at the window?' the boy asked.

'Now that I have no neighbours I'm nervous of burglars,' Aunt Hazel replied. 'The bars make me feel safe—a burglar would need a blowtorch to get in.'

'But he might come through the door.'

'Look.' She put a key into a keyhole close to the doorway and steel bars shot across it. 'I can operate the bars from the shop too, in case anyone tries to get through to the house in the daytime, and at night I'm as safe as a bank,' she said. 'It cost a lot to get them fitted but at my age you don't want to be worried each time the house creaks.

'That's enough of me—tell me about yourselves while you have your tea,' she added as she went to a cupboard which was stocked with cakes and biscuits.

She seemed so kind—rather like a nice granny—that the children found themselves telling her about their father being made redundant, how they did not get on with their stepmother, and how they would like to leave home. It was a great relief to talk about their problems to a sympathetic grown-up.

'She makes a change from Dora,' the boy whispered as they left her at the shop door, waving goodbye and telling them to visit her again.

'She likes you,' the girl said. 'All the time we were having tea and eating those gingerbread men she kept looking at you. Perhaps she wishes she'd been married and had a son.'

'I'm going to run away—to London,' he said suddenly.

The next few days were a nightmare for the girl. Her father looked ill and did not know what to do with himself except to go to the Job Centre each morning. Her brother was moody and silent and stayed away from school, and she was terrified that he would leave home without telling her.

One morning his stepmother found out that he was missing classes and there was an angry scene.

'You won't get any qualifications and you'll end up on the Unemployment like your father,' she yelled.

'Haven't we got enough trouble without you adding to it?' his father asked him.

The boy ran out of the house, slamming the door so hard that Dora's collection of china draught-horses rattled on the sideboard.

His sister left soon afterwards, and it seemed that the furious voices coming from the house followed her. She wanted to find her brother quickly because she knew how his mind worked, and she guessed that when he stormed out he had made his mind up never to return.

First she went to the cemetery, expecting that he would be paying a last visit before he hitch-hiked away from the grimy old town, but she found no one there. Then she was certain where he had gone, and in a few minutes she reached the canal.

The only living things she saw were two swans which, for some reason, made her think about Mr South and his fairy tales . . . something to do with the Swan Princess, she supposed. How she wished she lived in a fairy-tale land where all you had to worry about was dragons and ogres and wicked dwarfs—much better than real problems!

She was out of breath by the time she found herself in the demolished street where the sweet shop stood alone at the far end.

'Aunt Hazel,' she called when she went inside but there was no answer. It was the squawk of the parrot which made her open the door behind the counter and step into the living-room with its pretty furniture and barred windows.

To her horror she saw her brother in front of the open cupboard and he was *stealing*.

'How could you?' she gasped. 'And from such a nice old lady?'

'I'm not taking much,' he answered. 'Not money or anything—just some biscuits and scones to keep me going until I reach London.'

'It's still stealing,' she said. 'You should've asked.'

'I don't want anybody to talk me out of going,' he answered in a sulky voice. 'And that goes for you, too.'

She was about to give him an angry reply when there was a grating sound and the steel rods slid across the doorway behind her. Then Aunt Hazel appeared in the shop, her huge eyes peering at them through the bars as though they were animals in a zoo cage.

'Well, well, the chicks have returned to the gingerbread house,' she chuckled. 'Welcome back, Hansel and Gretel.'

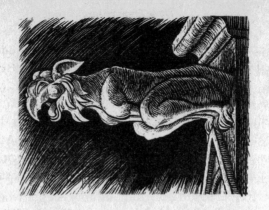

# Those Three Wishes

### ROBERT SCOTT

Her name was Melinda Alice. She was clever and pretty and very, very nasty. She was so nasty that all the other kids wanted to be friends with her. After all, it was better to be her friend than one of her victims.

Once, back in the Junior School, a new girl arrived in the middle of term. She was small and shy and wore glasses and, of course, she didn't have any friends. 'Connie,' Melinda Alice christened her. 'Connie, Connie, Connie—Yuk!'

'That's not my name. It's—'

'Connie,' insisted Melinda Alice. 'Short for Contamination,' she added, turning to her circle of friends. Then she touched the new girl on the shoulder and looked at her hand in disgust. 'Yuk! It's contaminated!' She held her hand out for the others to see then wiped it vigorously on her fresh, clean handkerchief, which she immediately dropped in the rubbish bin.

After that everything the new girl touched had to be avoided or cleaned thoroughly before anyone else would use it. After that, Melinda Alice was called Melinda Malice—but not when she might hear you.

Melinda Alice's mother worried about her but her father thought it was all part of growing up. And look how well she was doing. Indeed, Melinda Alice always got good grades and that, her father insisted, was what school was all about.

On this day Melinda Alice left for school early. There was going to be a maths test and she wanted to find a quiet corner where she could go over her books again. Being the best mattered to her. It gave her more power, especially with the teachers.

She had just turned up the lane to take the back way to school when she almost stepped on a snail making its slimy way across the path.

'Yuk! Gross!' She stopped and looked round for something to squash it with. What, after all, was one snail more or less. If it didn't want to be flattened it shouldn't get in the way. Not finding anything, she lifted her foot to stamp on it.

'Please don't,' said the snail.

'What!'

'Please don't stamp on me. I'll give you three wishes if you let me go.'

'Oh, yes,' said Melinda Alice. 'And where's your magic wand?'

'Try me,' said the snail. 'If you don't you'll never know what you missed.'

'OK,' said Melinda Alice. She always went in for competitions, arguing that if you didn't enter you couldn't possibly win. And if the snail didn't deliver she could always get him later. 'My first wish is: I wish . . . I wish I had pierced ears and small gold ear-rings.'

Melinda Alice had been pestering her parents for months. Her mother told her to ask her father and her father told her to wait until she was older. He was very firm about it and he wouldn't be bribed. But now—she felt her ears gently—now she had them anyway. She looked round for the snail but it had already disappeared.

It was then that she realized what enormous power she had. I can find a cure for cancer, she thought. I can make sure everyone has enough to eat and a house to live in. I can even stop wars. Could she? Could the snail really grant wishes like that?

Melinda Alice thought for a moment, then said, 'My second wish is: I wish I had a pair of roller-blades.' And suddenly she sat down hard on the path. 'Not here, stupid!' she shouted. 'Put them in my cupboard at home.' They disappeared. She made a mental note to check when she got home, but there was little doubt that the snail could make some wishes come true. She picked herself up. I can get my own back on people, she thought. All her fine ideas about saving the world had disappeared. I can be captain of all the school teams, I can come first in all the exams. I can have anything—*anything*—I want.

Melinda Alice smirked to herself. She had read fairy stories when she was small and she knew exactly what her third wish would be. After all, she would need lots of wishes if she was going to do everything she wanted.

It was then that she heard the bell. She was late. She would never make it in time. But she did, sliding into her place as her form teacher waited, then called her name.

'Thought you'd decided to give it a miss,' said a voice behind her.

'What do you mean?' She was panting, trying to recover her breath.

'The maths test. Thought you weren't going to bother.'

Melinda Alice's heart sank. The snail had made her late and she hadn't had time to study.

'Oh, no!' she groaned. 'I'll blow it. Oh, I wish I was dead!'

# Such a Sweet Little Girl

## LANCE SALWAY

It was at breakfast on a bright Saturday morning that Julie first made her announcement. She put down her spoon, swallowed a last mouthful of cornflakes and said, 'There's a ghost in my bedroom.'

No one took any notice. Her mother was writing a shopping list, and her father was deep in his newspaper. Neither of them heard what she said. Her brother Edward heard but he ignored her, which is what he usually did. Edward liked to pretend that Julie didn't exist. It wasn't easy, but he did his best.

Julie tried again. She raised her voice and said, 'There's a ghost in my bedroom.'

Mrs Bennett looked up from her list. 'Is there, dear? Oh, good. Do you think we need more marmalade? And I suppose I'd better buy a cake or something if your friends are coming to tea.'

Edward said sharply, 'Friends? What friends?'

'Sally and Rachel are coming to tea with Julie this afternoon,' his mother said.

44

Edward gave a loud theatrical groan. 'Oh, no. Why does she have to fill the house with her rotten friends?'

'You could fill the house with *your* friends, too,' Julie said sweetly. 'If you had any.'

Edward looked at her with loathing. 'Oh, I've got friends all right,' he said. 'I just don't inflict them on other people.'

'You haven't got any friends,' Julie said quietly. 'You haven't got any friends because no one likes you.'

'That's enough,' Mr Bennett said, looking up from his paper. There was silence then, broken only by the gentle rumble-slush, rumble-slush of the washing machine in the corner.

Edward chewed a piece of toast and thought how much he hated Julie. He hated a lot of people. Most people, in fact. But there were some he hated more than others. Mr Jenkins, who taught Maths. And that woman in the paper shop who'd accused him of stealing chewing gum, when everyone knew he never touched the stuff. And Julie. He hated Julie most of all.

He hated her pretty pale face, and her pretty fair curls, and her pretty little lisping voice. He hated the grown-ups who constantly fluttered round her, saying how enchanting she was, and so clever for her age, and wasn't Mrs Bennett lucky to have such a sweet little girl. What they didn't say, but he knew they were thinking behind their wide, bright smiles, was: poor Mrs Bennett with that lumpy sullen boy. So different from his sister. So different from lovely little Julie.

Lovely little Julie flung her spoon on the table. 'I *said* there's a ghost in my bedroom.'

Mrs Bennett put down her shopping list and ballpoint

in order to give Julie her full attention. 'Oh dear,' she said. 'I do hope it didn't frighten you, darling.'

Julie smiled and preened. 'No,' she said smugly. 'I wasn't frightened.'

Edward tried to shut his ears. He knew this dialogue by heart. The Bennett family spent a great deal of time adjusting their habits to suit Julie's fantasies. Once, for a whole month, they had all been forced to jump the bottom tread of the staircase because Julie insisted that two invisible rabbits were sleeping there. For a time she had been convinced, or so she said, that a pink dragon lived in the airing cupboard. And there had been a terrible few weeks the year before when all communication with her had to be conducted through an invisible fairy called Priscilla who lived on her left shoulder.

And now there was a ghost in her bedroom.

Try as he might, Edward couldn't shut out his sister's voice. On and on it whined: ' . . . I was really very brave and didn't run away even though it was so frightening, and I said . . . '

Edward looked at his parents with contempt. His father had put down the newspaper and was gazing at Julie with a soppy smile on his face. His mother was wearing the mock-serious expression that adults often adopt in order to humour their young. Edward hated them for it. If he'd told them a story about a ghost when *he* was seven, they'd have told him to stop being so silly, there's no such thing as ghosts, why don't you grow up, be a man.

'What sort of ghost is it?' he asked suddenly.

Julie looked at him in surprise. Then her eyes narrowed. 'It's a frightening ghost,' she said, 'with great big eyes and teeth and horrible, nasty claws. Big claws. And it smells.'

'Ghosts aren't like that,' Edward said scornfully. 'Ghosts have clanking chains and skeletons, and they carry their heads under their arms.'

'This ghost doesn't,' Julie snapped.

'Funny sort of ghost, then.'

'You don't know anything about it.'

Julie's voice was beginning to tremble. Edward sighed. There'd be tears soon and he'd get the blame. As usual.

'Come now, Edward,' his father said heartily. 'It's only pretend. Isn't it, lovey?'

Lovey shot him a vicious glance. 'It's *not* pretend. It's a real ghost. And it's in my bedroom.'

'Of course, darling.' Mrs Bennett picked up her shopping list again. 'How are we off for chutney, I wonder?'

But Edward wasn't going to let the matter drop. Not this time. 'Anyway,' he said, 'ghosts don't have claws.'

'This one does,' Julie said.

'Then you're lying.'

'I'm not. There *is* a ghost. I saw it.'

'Liar.'

'I'm not!' She was screaming now. 'I'll show you I'm not. I'll tell it to *get* you. With its claws. It'll come and get you with its claws.'

'Don't make me laugh.'

'*Edward!* That's *enough*!' His mother stood up and started to clear the table. 'Don't argue.'

'But there isn't a ghost,' Edward protested. 'There can't be!'

Mrs Bennett glanced uneasily at Julie. 'Of course there is,' she said primly. 'If Julie says so.'

'She's a liar, a nasty little liar.'

Julie kicked him hard under the table. Edward yelped,

and kicked back. Julie let out a screech, and then her face crumpled and she began to wail.

'*Now* look what you've done,' Mrs Bennett snapped. 'Oh *really*, Edward. You're twice her age. Why can't you leave her alone?'

'Because she's a liar, that's why.' Edward stood up and pushed his chair aside. 'Because there isn't a ghost in her bedroom. And even if there is, it won't have claws.' And he turned, and stormed out of the kitchen.

He came to a stop in the sitting-room, and crossed over to the window to see what sort of day it was going to be. Sunny, by the look of it. A small tightly cropped lawn lay in front of the house, a lawn that was identical in size and appearance to those in front of the other identical square brick houses which lined the road. Edward laughed out loud. Any ghost worthy of the name would wither away from boredom in such surroundings. No, there weren't any ghosts in Briarfield Gardens; with or without heads under their arms; with or without claws.

He turned away from the window. The day had started badly, thanks to Julie. And it would continue badly, thanks to Julie and her rotten friends who were coming to tea. And there was nothing he could do about it. Or was there? On the coffee table by the television set there lay a half-finished jigsaw puzzle. Julie had been working on it for ages, her fair curls bent earnestly over the table day after day. According to the picture on the box, the finished puzzle would reveal a thatched cottage surrounded by a flower-filled garden. When it was finished. If . . .

Edward walked across to the table and smashed the puzzle with one quick, practised movement of his hand. Pieces fell and flew and scattered on the carpet in a storm of coloured cardboard. And then he turned and ran upstairs to his room.

He hadn't long to wait. After a few minutes he heard the sounds that he was expecting. The kitchen door opening. A pause. Then a shrill, furious shriek, followed by loud sobbing. Running footsteps. A quieter comforting voice. Angry footsteps on the stairs. The rattling of the handle on his locked bedroom door. And then Julie's voice, not like a seven-year-old voice at all any more, but harsh and bitter with hate.

'The ghost'll get you, Edward. I'm going to tell it to get you. With its claws. With its horrible, sharp claws.'

And then, quite suddenly, Edward felt afraid.

The fear didn't last long. It had certainly gone by lunchtime, when Edward was given a ticking-off by his father for upsetting dear little Julie. And by the time Julie's friends arrived at four, he was quite his old self again.

'The ugly sisters are here!' he announced loudly as he opened the front door, having beaten Julie to it by a short head.

She glared at him, and quickly hustled Sally and Rachel up the stairs to her room.

Edward felt a bit guilty. Sally and Rachel weren't at all ugly. In fact, he quite liked them both. He ambled into the kitchen, where his mother was busy preparing tea.

She looked up when he came in. 'I do hope you're going to behave yourself this evening,' she said. 'We don't want a repetition of this morning's little episode, do we?'

'Well, she asked for it,' Edward said sullenly, and sneaked a biscuit from a pile on a plate.

'Hands off!' his mother said automatically. 'Julie did *not* ask for it. She was only pretending. You know what she's like. There was no need for you to be so nasty. And there was certainly no excuse for you to break up her jigsaw puzzle like that.'

Edward shuffled uneasily and stared at the floor.

'She *is* only seven, after all,' Mrs Bennett went on, slapping chocolate icing on a sponge cake as she did so. 'You must make allowances. The rest of us do.'

'She gets away with murder,' Edward mumbled. 'Just because she's such a sweet little girl.'

'Nonsense!' his mother said firmly. 'And keep your mucky paws off those ginger snaps. If anyone gets away with murder in this house, it's you.'

'But she can't really expect us to believe there's a ghost in her bedroom,' Edward said. 'Do *you* believe her? Come on, mum, do you?'

'I . . .' his mother began, and then she was interrupted by a familiar lisping voice.

'You *do* believe me, mummy, don't you?'

Julie was standing at the kitchen door. Edward wondered how long she'd been there. And how much she'd heard.

'Of course I do, darling,' Mrs Bennett said quickly. 'Now run along, both of you. Or I'll never have tea ready in time.'

Julie stared at Edward for a moment with her cold blue eyes, and then she went out of the kitchen as quietly as she'd entered it.

Tea passed off smoothly enough. Julie seemed to be on her best behaviour, but that was probably because her friends were there and she wanted to create a good impression. Edward followed her example. Julie didn't look at him or speak to him, but there was nothing unusual about that. She and the others chattered brightly about nothing in particular, and Edward said nothing at all.

It was dusk by the time they'd finished tea, and it was then that Julie suggested that they all play ghosts. She looked straight at Edward when she said this, and the proposal seemed like a challenge.

'Can anyone play?' he asked. 'Or is it just a game for horrible little girls?'

'Edward!' warned his mother.

'Of course you can play, Edward,' said Julie. 'You *must* play.'

'But not in the kitchen or the dining-room,' said Mrs Bennett. 'And keep out of our bedroom. I'll go and draw all the curtains and make sure the lights are switched off.'

'All right,' said Julie, and the other little girls clapped their hands with excitement.

'How do we play this stupid game?' asked Edward.

'Oh, it's easy,' said Julie. 'One of us is the ghost, and she has to frighten the others. If the ghost catches you and scares you, you have to scream and drop down on the floor. As if you were dead.'

'Like ''Murder in the Dark''?' asked Sally.

'Yes,' said Julie. 'Only we don't have a detective or anything like that.'

'It sounds a crummy game to me,' said Edward. 'I don't think I'll play.'

'Oh, *do*!' chorused Sally and Rachel. 'Please!'

And Julie came up to him and whispered, 'You *must* play, Edward. And don't forget what I said this morning; about my ghost, and how it's going to get you with its claws!'

'You must be joking!' Edward jeered. 'And anyway, I told you. Ghosts don't have claws.' He looked her straight in the eyes. 'Of course I'll play.'

Julie smiled, and then turned to the others and said, 'I'll be the ghost to start with. The rest of you run and hide. I'll count up to fifty and then I'll come and haunt you.'

Sally and Rachel galloped upstairs, squealing with excitement. Edward wandered into the hall, and stood for a moment wondering where to hide. It wasn't going to be easy. Their small brick box of a house didn't offer many possibilities. After a while he decided on the sitting-room. It was the most obvious place, and Julie would never think of looking there. He opened the door quietly, ducked down behind an armchair, and waited.

Silence settled over the house. Apart from washing-up sounds from the kitchen, all was quiet. Edward made himself comfortable on the carpet, and waited for the distant screams that would tell him that Sally had been discovered, or Rachel. But no sounds came. As he waited, ears straining against the silence, the room grew darker. The day was fading and it would soon be night.

And then, suddenly, Edward heard a slight noise near the door. His heart leaped and, for some reason, his mouth went dry. And then the fear returned, the unaccountable fear he had felt that morning when Julie hissed her threat through his bedroom door.

The air seemed much colder now, but that could only be his imagination, surely. But he knew that he wasn't imagining the wild thumping of his heart, or the sickening lurching of his stomach. He remembered Julie's words and swallowed hard.

'The ghost'll get you, Edward. With its claws. With its sharp, horrible claws.'

He heard sounds again, closer this time. A scuffle. Whispering. Or was it whispering? Someone was there. Something. He tried to speak, but gave only a curious croak. 'Julie?' he said. 'I know you're there. I know it's you.'

Silence. A dark terrible silence. And then the light snapped on and the room was filled with laughter and shouts of, 'Got you! Caught you! The ghost has caught you!' He saw Julie's face alive with triumph and delight, and, behind her, Sally and Rachel grinning, and the fear was replaced by an anger far darker and more intense than the terror he'd felt before.

'Edward's scared of the ghost!' Julie jeered. 'Edward's a scaredy cat! He's frightened! He's frightened of the gho-ost!'

'I'm not!' Edward shouted. 'I'm not scared! There isn't a ghost!' He pushed past Julie and ran out of the room and up the stairs. He'd show her. He'd prove she didn't have a ghost. There were no such things as ghosts. She didn't have a ghost in her room. She didn't.

Julie's bedroom was empty. Apart from the furniture and the pictures and the toys and dolls and knick-knacks. He opened the wardrobe and pulled shoes and games out on to the floor. He burrowed in drawers, scattering books and stuffed animals and clothes around him. At last he stopped, gasping for breath. And turned.

His mother was standing in the doorway, staring at him in amazement. Clustered behind her were the puzzled, anxious faces of Sally and Rachel. And behind them, Julie, looking at him with her ice-blue eyes.

'What on earth are you doing?' his mother asked.

'See?' he panted. 'There isn't a ghost here. She hasn't got a ghost in her bedroom. There's nothing here. Nothing.'

'Isn't there?' said Julie. 'Are you sure you've looked properly?'

Sally—or was it Rachel?—gave a nervous giggle.

'That's enough,' said Mrs Bennett. 'Now I suggest you tidy up the mess you've made in here, Edward, and then go to your room.. I don't know why you're behaving so strangely. But it's got to stop. It's got to.'

She turned and went downstairs. Sally and Rachel followed her. Julie lingered by the door and stared mockingly at Edward. He stared back.

'It's still here, you know,' she said at last. 'The ghost is still here. And it'll get you.'

'You're a dirty little liar!' he shouted. 'A nasty, filthy little liar!'

Julie gaped at him for a moment, taken aback by the force of his rage. Then, 'It'll get you!' she screamed. 'With its claws. Its horrible claws. It'll get you tonight. When you're asleep. Because I hate you. I hate you. Yes, it'll *really* get you. Tonight.'

It was dark when Edward awoke. At first he didn't know where he was. And then he remembered. He was in bed. In his bedroom. It was the middle of the night. And he remembered, too, Julie's twisted face and the things she said. The face and the words had kept him awake, and had haunted his dreams when at last he slept.

It was ridiculous, really. All this fuss about an imaginary ghost. Why did he get in such a state over Julie? She was only a little kid after all. His baby sister. You were supposed to love your sister—not fear her. But no, he wasn't *really* afraid of her. How could he be? Such a sweet little girl with blue eyes and fair bouncing curls who was half his age. A little girl who played games and imagined things. Who imagined ghosts. A ghost in her bedroom.

But he *was* frightened. He knew that now. And as his fear mounted again, the room seemed to get colder. He shut his eyes and snuggled down under the blankets, shutting out the room and the cold. But not the fear.

And then he heard it. A sound. A faint, scraping sound, as though something heavy was being dragged along the landing. A sound that came closer and grew louder. A wet, slithering sound. And with it came a smell, a sickening smell of drains and dead leaves and decay. And the sound grew louder and he could hear breathing, harsh breathing, long choking breaths coming closer.

'Julie?' Edward said, and then he repeated it louder. 'Julie!'

But there was no answer. All he heard was the scraping, dragging sound coming closer, closer. Near his door now. Closer.

'I know it's you!' Edward shouted, and he heard the fear in his own voice. 'You're playing ghosts again, aren't you? Aren't you?'

And then there was silence. No sound at all. Edward sat up in bed and listened. The awful slithering noise had stopped. It had gone. The ghost had gone.

He hugged himself with relief. It had been a dream, that's all. He'd imagined it. Just as Julie imagined things. Imagined ghosts.

Then he heard the breathing again. The shuddering, choking breaths. And he knew that the thing hadn't gone. That it was still there. Outside his door. Waiting. Waiting.

And Edward screamed, 'Julie! Stop it! Stop it! Please stop it! I believe you! I believe in the ghost!'

The door opened. The shuddering breaths seemed to fill the room, and the smell, and the slithering wet sound of a shape. Something was coming towards him, something huge and dark and . . .

He screamed as the claws, yes, the claws tore at his hands, his chest, his face. And he screamed again as the darkness folded over him.

When Julie woke up and came downstairs the ambulance had gone. Her mother was sitting alone in the kitchen, looking pale and frightened. She smiled weakly when she saw Julie, and then frowned.

'Darling,' she said. 'I did so hope you wouldn't wake up. I didn't want you to be frightened . . .'

'What's the matter, mummy?' asked Julie. 'Why are you crying?'

Her mother smiled again, and drew Julie to her, folding her arms around her so that she was warm and safe. 'You must be very brave, darling,' she said. 'Poor Edward has been hurt. We don't know what happened but he's been very badly hurt.'

'Hurt? What do you mean, mummy?'

Her mother brushed a stray curl from the little girl's face. 'We don't know what happened, exactly. Something attacked him. His face . . . ' Her voice broke then, and she looked away quickly. 'He has been very badly scratched. They're not sure if his eyes . . . ' She stopped and fumbled in her dressing-gown pocket for a tissue.

'I expect my ghost did it,' Julie said smugly.

'What did you say, dear?'

Julie looked up at her mother. 'My ghost did it. I told it to. I told it to hurt Edward because I hate him. The ghost hurt him. The ghost in my bedroom.'

Mrs Bennett stared at Julie. 'This is no time for games,' she said. 'We're very upset. Your father's gone to the hospital with Edward. We don't know if . . . ' Her eyes filled with tears. 'I'm in no mood for your silly stories about ghosts, Julie. Not now. I'm too upset.'

'But it's true,' Julie said. 'My ghost *did* do it. Because I told it to.'

Mrs Bennett pushed her away and stood up. 'All right, Julie, that's enough. Back to bed now. You can play your games tomorrow.'

'But it's not a game,' Julie persisted. 'It's true! My ghost . . . '

And then she saw the angry expression on her mother's face, and she stopped. Instead, she snuggled up to her and whispered, 'I'm sorry, mummy. You're right. I *was* pretending. I was only pretending about the ghost. There isn't a ghost in my room. I was making it all up. And I'm so sorry about poor Edward.'

Mrs Bennett relaxed and smiled and drew Julie to her once again. 'That's my baby,' she said softly. 'That's my sweet little girl. Of course you were only pretending. Of course there wasn't a ghost. Would I let a nasty ghost come and frighten my little girl? Would I? Would I?'

'No, mummy,' said Julie. 'Of course you wouldn't.'

'Off you go to bed now.'

'Goodnight, mummy,' said Julie.

'Sleep well, my pet,' said her mother.

And Julie walked out of the kitchen and into the hall and the stairs to her bedroom. She went inside, and closed the door behind her.

And the ghost came out to meet her.

'She doesn't believe me, either,' Julie said. 'We'll have to show her, won't we? Just as we showed Edward.'

And the ghost smiled, and nodded. And they sat down together, Julie and the ghost, and decided what they would do.

# Ghost Hunter

### SYDNEY J. BOUNDS

I t was already dark when Peter Matson turned into St Agnes Road looking for a house named *Rosemont*. The bright beam from his cycle headlamp swept across tall houses, some down at heel and others given a lick of paint and turned into flats.

*Rosemont* lurked behind leafless trees, a large, rambling building with high brick chimney stacks and gables. It appeared to have had a lot of extensions built on to it at different times. Peter thought it an unusual house to find in a London suburb, like something out of 'Dracula'.

A single light gleamed from a downstairs window as he swung into the short drive. He saw a wooden porch and a large black door and, carved into the stonework above, a date: 1882.

Peter dismounted and leaned his cycle against the porch. His legs ached and a chill wind from the dark trees froze the sweat on his body. It had been a long ride and his saddle-bags were weighted down with all his equipment.

He used the old brass knocker to announce his arrival. Footsteps echoed inside and the door opened.

Peter faced a tubby man in a tweed suit; his hair was a fringe of grey about an egg-bald head, and he looked worried.

'Mr Swann? I'm Peter Matson. Sorry I'm a bit late, but the ride took longer than I expected.'

'Better late than never. Come on in.' Swann glanced at his watch as Peter wheeled his bike inside. 'I'll have to leave almost immediately—my wife's waiting for me.'

Marble-blue eyes looked with curiosity at Peter's lanky frame, his studious expression and thick-lensed glasses. In windcheater and jeans he looked no more than sixteen.

'You'll be all right here, alone?'

Peter smiled as he shut the door. 'I'm not afraid, if that's what you mean.'

'No, I suppose not—or you wouldn't be a member of a ghost hunting agency. I'd thought of exorcism, of course, but we don't want that kind of publicity. We hope you'll be discreet.'

'Of course. We don't want publicity either.'

It was cold in the hall and dust had gathered in the corners.

'This place is a bit of a maze,' Swann said, leading the way. 'I've just time to show you around.'

A passage branched off to the right, turned left into a large bare room and continued again as a corridor. Swann switched on lights as he went.

'Here's the kitchen. Make tea or coffee if you like.'

Swann retraced his steps to the entrance hall. 'All the doors and windows are locked. There's a cellar downstairs—that's the boiler room.'

They went up the wide, sweeping staircase. At the top was an open door leading to other rooms, and a passageway branching away to the left.

'You can walk right round on this floor,' the estate agent said. 'All the rooms are connected.'

Peter tried to form a mental map of the building, but the place really did seem a maze. He followed Swann along a passage that went up a short flight of stairs and down again, through an L-shaped room that ended in another corridor.

Finally they arrived at the end of a branch passage and the bottom of a steep flight of stairs that angled off to the right.

Swann paused. 'I don't believe it myself, but I'm told that some people see things about here.'

Peter looked up the bare wooden staircase as Swann switched on a dim light. 'What's up there?'

'Just attics. I suppose they were servants' quarters. Junk rooms.' Swann's tone of voice changed. 'I hope you can clear up this business. I can't get clients interested at all—the place has a bad name. Something so scared the previous tenants that they moved out.'

'I'm glad of the chance to investigate a haunting,' Peter said earnestly.

'So you do believe in ghosts?'

'I try to keep an open mind. Strange things happen . . . but ghosts, meaning spirits of the dead . . . ?' Peter shrugged. 'We're still looking for the evidence.'

His voice dropped to a murmur, as if he were speaking more to himself than to Swann. 'If ghosts are the spirits of the dead, how do they feel about the after-life? What does it feel like to be a ghost? Can a ghost feel anything at all?'

Swann wasn't interested. 'I've got to run. Just make yourself at home.'

'I'm curious,' Peter said quickly. 'Is there a story behind this haunting?'

'Nothing much. The whole thing's a mystery. A young girl committed suicide here, so they say. Nobody really knows.'

Peter followed him downstairs and the estate agent gave him a spare key. He made sure the front door was locked. Alone in the old house, he went round checking doors and windows. He sealed thread across them and left the passage lights on.

Then he unpacked his saddle-bags and assembled his ghost hunting equipment, setting up tape recorders and automatic cameras. He slipped a torch into his pocket.

He returned to the kitchen and made himself coffee. Relaxed in a chair, he sipped slowly and listened to the sounds of the house: the creaking of timbers and crack of water pipes, the rattle of a window.

Suddenly he sat up straight in his chair, sniffing the air. He put down his mug and stepped into the passage. No, he hadn't imagined it; he could smell a woman's perfume above the aroma of coffee. In the passage it appeared stronger. There was nothing subtle about it, just a reek of cheap scent.

Peter moved along the corridor, opening doors to make sure that each room was empty. He ended back in the main hallway. Here the perfume was almost overpowering, saturating the air.

He stared up the wide, curving staircase; in the bend he thought he detected something grey, some slight suggestion of movement. But he wasn't sure.

As he placed a foot on the lower step, the perfume

vanished. His ears caught a soft laugh, so soft he couldn't be certain he hadn't imagined it.

Then there was nothing; no perfume, no hint of movement, no laughter. He froze for a long moment, then darted quickly up the stairs and searched each room. He found no one.

Peter hummed a happy tune. He was sure now that he wasn't wasting his time.

When Swann opened the door the next evening, he asked: 'Any luck?'

'Oh yes, we've got something here.'

The estate agent brightened at once. 'Then you'll be able to do something about it?'

'It depends,' Peter said cautiously. 'I can't guarantee anything.'

'It's like this,' Swann confided. 'I've got Head Office breathing down my neck. They're not interested in excuses, only sales. If I can't sell this place soon, it's going to count against me.'

'Stick it out,' Peter advised. 'A haunting of this kind doesn't usually last long.'

After Swann left, Peter arranged his tape recorders and cameras at the top and bottom of the main staircase. He filled a thermos flask with coffee and moved a chair into the hall, placing himself where he could watch the bend in the stairs.

The hours passed slowly before the soft laugh was repeated. Peter came alert immediately. He rose from his chair and padded to the foot of the stairs. The provocative sound came again from somewhere above, and he heard the tap-tap of high-heeled shoes going up.

And still he saw no one. The skin tightened on his scalp, lifting his hair, as the tapping sounds receded.

Peter found he had to take a grip on his nerves before he could go up but, finally, he forced himself to climb to the top of the stairs.

He looked down the branch passage to the left and, at the far end, glimpsed a wraithlike figure. It was an image of a girl of about seventeen or eighteen, and translucent— or so it seemed, because he could see the wall behind her. He hurried forward, and the image vanished as if a veil had dropped between them.

Peter studied the walls closely, rapping here and there. Solid. He inspected the adjoining rooms and found no sign of trickery. He went back downstairs and re-ran his tapes; the laughter and sound of high heels were there, faint but definitely recorded.

The following evening was a Friday, and Swann was going away for the weekend. Peter played the tapes for him and said: 'I've developed my film and there's nothing on it. But this sort of freak happening is not unusual.'

The estate agent regarded him with a curious expression. 'You do realize you'll be quite alone here till Monday morning? Are you sure you'll be all right?'

Peter nodded. 'I'm not worried. Perhaps, with peace and quiet for forty-eight hours, our ghost will reveal herself.'

Swann shrugged and left rather hurriedly.

Peter patrolled the building before taking up his post on the first floor, at the point where the ghost had vanished. But if he had expected any quick revelation he was disappointed. *Rosemont* cooled and creaked as he nodded in his chair.

He came to, startled, as a feminine voice purred in his ear. 'Soon . . . soon, now . . .'

He was cold, and his legs were stiff as broomsticks.

He glimpsed the ghost-girl, distant, along the passage to the right. He rose and moved towards her. The image lingered as if waiting for him, then retreated, high heels tap-tapping, to the foot of the staircase leading to the attics. She seemed more solid than the previous night.

She went up the flight of steep narrow stairs, reached the top and paused to look down at him. As Peter started up after her, she disappeared.

He went up, holding tight to the bannister rail. Moonlight, filtering through dusty windows, gave a pale glow that threw grey shadows. He had little doubt that she had deliberately led him up here, and wondered why. He made a quick search of the attics but discovered nothing out of the ordinary.

He spent most of Saturday searching the attics thoroughly. He carried his cameras and tape recorders to the top floor, tested and placed them carefully. He had the old house entirely to himself.

There were three small rooms with bare walls and floorboards thick with dust. The room furthest from the stairs still had some junk in it: broken furniture, ancient newspapers, a cracked mirror on the wall.

If the ghost had lured him to this topmost floor for some revelation, she had nowhere left to go.

Peter wrote a report for his agency and went out for a meal. He left it late before returning because, on the previous night, nothing much had happened before midnight. He let himself in and stood listening to the house. Then he went upstairs, switching on passage lights as he went.

He paused at the foot of the narrow stairs leading to the attics. Should he wait at the bottom? Or go straight up? He mentally tossed a coin, decided to play the game her way and allow her to lure him up the stairs.

He moved a chair into position and settled down for his vigil. This time he did not have long to wait for her; perhaps she, too, was eager for the final confrontation.

Her crude perfume came first, alerting him. Then the old house became silent; the hush had a peculiar deadness to it, as if any sound were no longer possible.

As he stared up the shadowed stairway she appeared at the top, smiling down at him. It was a smile of invitation. She seemed as real as any flesh-and-blood girl, and his pulse beat faster.

As he went carefully up the stairs, Peter told himself she was not real. The old treads were narrow and made no sound. She waited for him in silent stillness, allowing him to approach.

She was young, with an air of glamour, and her heavy scent acted like a drug.

When he reached the top, she backed away along the short passage to the last room of all. The moonlight was strong and bright, and she cast no shadow. Yet he saw her as plainly as any living girl.

She backed up against the far wall of the tiny room until she could go no further. Peter stood in the doorway and there were only yards between them.

The mirror showed only Peter's reflection. His breath made no sound.

Her eyes were dark pits in the pale oval of her face, and her gaze was riveted on him, compelling, almost hypnotic. He felt strangely reluctant to move as she left the wall and glided towards him.

She came closer, closer, till it seemed he sensed hot breath on his face. She wrapped her arms about him, and he felt the pressure of her embrace. Her hands pressed against his back, and he was engulfed in a cloud of sultry perfume.

Her mouth fastened eagerly on his. It was cold—deadly cold. Her kiss turned into a dreadful noiseless sucking and, too late, he began to struggle. The illusion of solid flesh ended. Only the mouth was real, frighteningly real, sucking . . .

Brightness exploded like a flash-bulb. Sounds rushed in at him, the creak of old timbers, the rattle of a window.

Sight returned slowly. By moonlight, the attic room appeared misty and insubstantial.

The ghost-girl had gone, and he saw another Peter walk towards the door. This other Peter paused on the threshold to look back, and his lips curved in a smile of triumph. The laugh which followed was hauntingly familiar.

Peter Matson looked down at himself and discovered that he no longer had a body. The spirit of the dead girl had stolen it. He cried out but had no voice. Terror seized him as he heard feet clatter down the stairs.

Now he knew how it felt to be a ghost. He moved and made no footfalls. He drifted through a wall. Nothing was real; he had lost all sense of touch. He sank through the floor.

Tears welled in his eyes that were not there, but they still blinded him. He heard the front door slam and watched the new Peter cycle away. Silence came to *Rosemont*.

When the estate agent visited the house on Monday morning, there was no sign of Peter Matson. His equipment and cycle were gone.

Swann was disgusted; the ghost hunter had left without a word. Well, he'd have something to say about that when he phoned the agency.

He stayed just long enough to make sure everything was locked up—and, for the first time, felt uneasy in the old house.

Could *Rosemont* be haunted?

Something just beyond the corner of his eye seemed to follow him, and a noise echoed in his head.

'Help me . . . help me!'

Swann left in a hurry, slamming the door behind him, suddenly nervous. That voice . . . why did he imagine the voice in his head sounded like young Peter Matson?

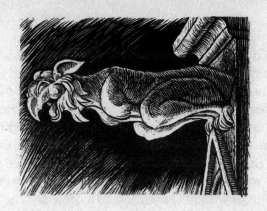

# Thus I Refute Beelzy

### JOHN COLLIER

'There goes the tea bell,' said Mrs Carter. 'I hope Simon hears it.'

They looked out from the window of the drawing room. The long garden, agreeably neglected, ended in a waste plot. Here a little summerhouse was passing close by beauty on its way to complete decay. This was Simon's retreat. It was almost completely screened by the tangled branches of the apple tree and the pear tree, planted too close together, as they always are in the suburbs. They caught a glimpse of him now and then, as he strutted up and down, mouthing and gesticulating, performing all the solemn mumbo jumbo of small boys who spend long afternoons at the forgotten ends of long gardens.

'There he is, bless him!' said Betty.

'Playing his game,' said Mrs Carter. 'He won't play with the other children any more. And if I go down there—the temper! And comes in tired out!'

'He doesn't have his sleep in the afternoons?' asked Betty.

'You know what Big Simon's ideas are,' said Mrs Carter. ' "Let him choose for himself," he says. That's what he chooses, and he comes in as white as a sheet.'

'Look! He's heard the bell,' said Betty. The expression was justified, though the bell had ceased ringing a full minute ago. Small Simon stopped in his parade exactly as if its tinny dingle had at that moment reached his ear. They watched him perform certain ritual sweeps and scratchings with his little stick, and come lagging over the hot and flaggy grass towards the house.

Mrs Carter led the way down to the playroom, or garden-room, which was also the tea-room for hot days. It had been the huge scullery of this tall Georgian house. Now the walls were cream-washed, there was coarse blue net in the windows, canvas-covered armchairs on the stone floor, and a reproduction of Van Gogh's *Sunflowers* over the mantelpiece.

Small Simon came drifting in, and accorded Betty a perfunctory greeting. His face was an almost perfect triangle, pointed at the chin, and he was paler than he should have been. 'The little elf-child!' cried Betty.

Simon looked at her. 'No,' said he.

At that moment the door opened, and Mr Carter came in, rubbing his hands. He was a dentist, and washed them before and after everything he did. 'You!' said his wife. 'Home already!'

'Not unwelcome, I hope,' said Mr Carter, nodding to Betty. 'Two people cancelled their appointments; I decided to come home. I said, I hope I am not unwelcome.'

'Silly!' said his wife. 'Of course not.'

'Small Simon seems doubtful,' continued Mr Carter. 'Small Simon, are you sorry to see me at tea with you?'

'No, Daddy.'

'No, what?'

'No, Big Simon.'

'That's right. Big Simon and Small Simon. That sounds more like friends, doesn't it? At one time, little boys had to call their father ''sir''. If they forgot—a good spanking. On the bottom, Small Simon! On the bottom!' said Mr Carter, washing his hands once more with his invisible soap and water.

The little boy turned crimson with shame or rage.

'But now, you see,' said Betty, to help, 'you can call your father whatever you like.'

'And what,' asked Mr Carter, 'has Small Simon been doing this afternoon? While Big Simon has been at work.'

'Nothing,' muttered his son.

'Then you have been bored,' said Mr Carter. 'Learn from experience, Small Simon. Tomorrow, do something amusing, and you will not be bored. I want him to learn from experience, Betty. That is my way, the new way.'

'I have learned,' said the boy, speaking like an old, tired man, as little boys so often do.

'It would hardly seem so,' said Mr Carter, 'if you sit on your behind all the afternoon, doing nothing. Had *my* father caught me doing nothing, I should not have sat very comfortably.'

'He played,' said Mrs Carter.

'A bit,' said the boy, shifting on his chair.

'Too much,' said Mrs Carter. 'He comes in all nervy and dazed. He ought to have his rest.'

'He is six,' said her husband. 'He is a reasonable being. He must choose for himself. But what game is this, Small Simon, that is worth getting nervy and dazed over? There are very few games as good as all that.'

'It's nothing,' said the boy.

'Oh, come,' said his father. 'We are friends, are we not? You can tell me. I was a Small Simon once, just like you, and played the same games you play. Of course, there were no aeroplanes in those days. With whom do you play this fine game? Come on, we must all answer civil questions, or the world would never go round. With whom do you play?'

'Mr Beelzy,' said the boy, unable to resist.

'Mr Beelzy?' said his father, raising his eyebrows enquiringly at his wife.

'It's a game he makes up,' she said.

'Not makes up!' cried the boy. 'Fool!'

'That is telling stories,' said his mother. 'And rude as well. We had better talk of something different.'

'No wonder he is rude,' said Mr Carter, 'if you say he tells lies, and then insist on changing the subject. He tells you his fantasy; you implant a guilt feeling. What can you expect? A defence mechanism. Then you get a real lie.'

'Like in *These Three*,' said Betty. 'Only different, of course. *She* was an unblushing little liar.'

'I would have made her blush,' said Mr Carter, 'in the proper part of her anatomy. But Small Simon is in the fantasy stage. Are you not, Small Simon? You just make things up.'

'No, I don't,' said the boy.

'You do,' said his father. 'And because you do, it is not too late to reason with you. There is no harm in a fantasy, old chap. There is nothing wrong with a bit of make-believe. Only you must learn the difference between daydreams and real things, or your brain will never grow. It will never be the brain of a Big Simon. So, come on.

Let us hear about this Mr Beelzy of yours. Come on. What is he like?'

'He isn't like anything,' said the boy.

'Like nothing on earth?' said his father. 'That's a terrible fellow.'

'I'm not frightened of him,' said the child, smiling. 'Not a bit.'

'I should hope not,' said his father. 'If you were, you would be frightening yourself. I am always telling people, older people than you are, that they are just frightening themselves. Is he a funny man? Is he a giant?'

'Sometimes he is,' said the little boy.

'Sometimes one thing, sometimes another,' said his father. 'Sounds pretty vague. Why can't you tell us just what he's like?'

'I love him,' said the small boy. 'He loves me.'

'That's a big word,' said Mr Carter. 'That might be better kept for real things, like Big Simon and Small Simon.'

'He is real,' said the boy, passionately. 'He's not a fool. He's real.'

'Listen,' said his father. 'When you go down the garden there's nobody there. Is there?'

'No,' said the boy.

'Then you think of him, inside your head, and he comes.'

'No,' said Small Simon. 'I have to make marks. On the ground. With my stick.'

'That doesn't matter.'

'Yes, it does.'

'Small Simon, you are being obstinate,' said Mr Carter. 'I am trying to explain something to you. I have been longer in the world than you have, so naturally I am older

73

and wiser. I am explaining that Mr Beelzy is a fantasy of yours. Do you hear? Do you understand?'

'Yes, Daddy.'

'He is a game. He is a let's-pretend.'

The little boy looked down at his plate, smiling resignedly.

'I hope you are listening to me,' said his father. 'All you have to do is to say, "I have been playing a game of let's-pretend. With someone I make up, called Mr Beelzy." Then no one will say you tell lies, and you will know the difference between dreams and reality. Mr Beelzy is a daydream.'

The little boy still stared at his plate.

'He is sometimes there and sometimes not there,' pursued Mr Carter. 'Sometimes he's like one thing, sometimes another. You can't really see him. Not as you see me. I am real. You can't touch him. You can touch me. I can touch you.' Mr Carter stretched out his big, white dentist's hand, and took his little son by the nape of the neck. He stopped speaking for a moment and tightened his hand. The little boy sank his head still lower.

'Now you know the difference,' said Mr Carter, 'between a pretend and a real thing. You and I are one thing; he is another. Which is the pretend? Come on. Answer me. Which is the pretend?'

'Big Simon and Small Simon,' said the little boy.

'Don't!' cried Betty, and at once put her hand over her mouth, for why should a visitor cry, 'Don't!' when a father is explaining things in a scientific and modern way? Besides, it annoys the father.

'Well, my boy,' said Mr Carter, 'I have said you must be allowed to learn from experience. Go upstairs. Right up to your room. You shall learn whether it is better to reason, or to be perverse and obstinate. Go up. I shall follow you.'

'You are not going to beat the child?' cried Mrs Carter.

'No,' said the little boy. 'Mr Beelzy won't let him.'

'Go on up with you!' shouted his father.

Small Simon stopped at the door. 'He said he wouldn't let anyone hurt me,' he whimpered. 'He said he'd come like a lion, with wings on, and eat them up.'

'You'll learn how real he is!' shouted his father after him. 'If you can't learn it at one end, you shall learn it at the other. I'll have your breeches down. I shall finish my cup of tea first, however,' said he to the two women.

Neither of them spoke. Mr Carter finished his tea, and unhurriedly left the room, washing his hands with his invisible soap and water.

Mrs Carter said nothing. Betty could think of nothing to say. She wanted to be talking for she was afraid of what they might hear.

Suddenly it came. It seemed to tear the air apart. 'Good God!' she cried. 'What was that? He's hurt him.' She sprang out of her chair, her silly eyes flashing behind her glasses. 'I'm going up there!' she cried, trembling.

'Yes, let us go up,' said Mrs Carter. 'Let us go up. That was not Small Simon.'

It was on the second-floor landing that they found the shoe, with the man's foot still in it, much like that last morsel of a mouse which sometimes falls unnoticed from the side of the jaws of the cat.

# *Voodoo*

## FREDRIC BROWN

Mr Decker's wife had just returned from a trip to Haiti—a trip she had taken alone—to give them a cooling off period before they discussed a divorce.

It hadn't worked. Neither of them had cooled off in the slightest. In fact, they were finding now that they hated one another more than ever.

'Half,' said Mrs Decker firmly. 'I'll not settle for anything less than half the money plus half of the property.'

'Ridiculous!' said Mr Decker.

'Is it? I could have it all, you know. And quite easily, too. I studied voodoo while in Haiti.'

'Rot!' said Mr Decker.

'It isn't. And you should be glad that I am a good woman for I could kill you quite easily if I wished. I would then have *all* the money and *all* the real estate, and without any fear of consequences. A death accomplished by voodoo cannot be distinguished from a death by heart failure.'

'Rubbish!' said Mr Decker.

'You think so? I have wax and a hatpin. Do you want to give me a tiny pinch of your hair or a fingernail clipping or two—that's all I need—and let me show you?'

'Nonsense!' said Mr Decker.

'Then why are you afraid to have me try? Since *I* know it works, I'll make you a proposition. If it doesn't kill you, I'll give you a divorce and ask for nothing. If it does, I'll get it all automatically.'

'Done!' said Mr Decker. 'Get your wax and hatpin.' He glanced at his fingernails. 'Pretty short. I'll give you a bit of hair.'

When he came back with a few short strands of hair in the lid of an aspirin tin, Mrs Decker had already started softening the wax. She kneaded the hair into it, then shaped it into the rough effigy of a human being.

'You'll be sorry,' she said, and thrust the hatpin into the chest of the wax figure.

Mr Decker was surprised, but he was more pleased than sorry. He had not believed in voodoo, but being a cautious man he never took chances.

Besides, it had always irritated him that his wife so seldom cleaned her hairbrush.

# The Near Departed

### RICHARD MATHESON

The small man opened the door and stepped in out of the glaring sunlight. He was in his early fifties, a spindly, plain-looking man with receding grey hair. He closed the door without a sound, then stood in the shadowy foyer, waiting for his eyes to adjust to the change in light. He was wearing a black suit, white shirt, and black tie. His face was pale and dry skinned despite the heat of the day.

When his eyes had refocused themselves, he removed his panama hat and moved along the hallway to the office, his black shoes soundless on the carpeting.

The mortician looked up from his desk. 'Good afternoon,' he said.

'Good afternoon.' The small man's voice was soft.

'Can I help you?'

'Yes, you can,' the small man said.

The mortician gestured to the armchair on the other side of his desk. 'Please.'

The small man perched on the edge of the chair and

set the panama hat on his lap. He watched the mortician open a drawer and remove a printed form.

'Now,' the mortician said. He withdrew a black pen from its onyx holder. 'Who is the deceased?' he asked gently.

'My wife,' the small man said.

The mortician made a sympathetic noise. 'I'm sorry,' he said.

'Yes.' The small man gazed at him blankly.

'What is her name?' the mortician asked.

'Marie,' the small man answered quietly. 'Arnold.'

The mortician wrote the name. 'Address?' he asked.

The small man told him.

'Is she there now?' the mortician asked.

'She's there,' the small man said.

The mortician nodded.

'I want everything perfect,' the small man said. 'I want the best you have.'

'Of course,' the mortician said. 'Of course.'

'Cost is unimportant,' said the small man. His throat moved as he swallowed drily. 'Everything is unimportant now. Except for this.'

'I understand,' the mortician said.

'I want the best you have,' the small man said. 'She's beautiful. She has to have the very best.'

'I understand.'

'She always had the best. I saw to it.'

'Of course.'

'There'll be many people,' said the small man. 'Everybody loved her. She's so beautiful. So young. She has to have the very best. You understand?'

'Absolutely,' the mortician reassured him. 'You'll be more than satisfied, I guarantee you.'

'She's so beautiful,' the small man said. 'So young.'

'I'm sure,' the mortician said.

The small man sat without moving as the mortician asked him questions. His voice did not vary in tone as he spoke. His eyes blinked so infrequently the mortician never saw them doing it.

When the form was completed, the small man signed and stood. The mortician stood and walked around the desk. 'I guarantee you you'll be satisfied,' he said, his hand extended.

The small man took his hand and gripped it momentarily. His palm was dry and cool.

'We'll be over at your house within the hour,' the mortician told him.

'Fine,' the small man said.

The mortician walked beside him down the hallway.

'I want everything perfect for her,' the small man said. 'Nothing but the very best.'

'Everything will be exactly as you wish.'

'She deserves the best.' The small man stared ahead. 'She's so beautiful,' he said. 'Everybody loved her. Everybody. She's so young and beautiful.'

'When did she die?' the mortician asked.

The small man didn't seem to hear. He opened the door and stepped into the sunlight, putting on his panama hat. He was half-way to his car when he replied, a faint smile on his lips, 'As soon as I get home.'

# An Alpine Divorce

## ROBERT BARR

I n some natures there are no halftones; nothing but
raw primary colours. John Bodman was a man who
was always at one extreme or the other. This probably
would have mattered little had he not married a wife
whose nature was an exact duplicate of his own.

Doubtless there exists in this world precisely the right
woman for any given man to marry, and vice versa; but
when you consider that a human being has the opportunity of
being acquainted with only a few hundred people, and
out of the few hundred that there are but a dozen or less
whom he knows intimately, and out of the dozen, one or
two friends at most, it will easily be seen, when we
remember the number of millions who inhabit this world,
that probably, since the earth was created, the right man
has never yet met the right woman. The mathematical
chances are all against such a meeting, and this is the
reason that divorce courts exist. Marriage at best is but a
compromise, and if two people happen to be united who
are of an uncompromising nature there is trouble.

In the lives of these two people there was no middle distance. The result was bound to be either love or hate, and in the case of Mr and Mrs Bodman it was hate of the most bitter and arrogant kind.

In some parts of the world incompatibility of temper is considered a just cause for obtaining a divorce, but in England no such subtle distinction is made, and so, until the wife became a criminal, or the man became both criminal and cruel, these two were linked together by a bond that only death could sever. Nothing can be worse than this state of things, and the matter was only made the more hopeless by the fact that Mrs Bodman lived a blameless life, and her husband was no worse, but rather better, than the majority of men. Perhaps, however, that statement held only up to a certain point, for John Bodman had reached a state of mind in which he resolved to get rid of his wife at all hazards. If he had been a poor man he would probably have deserted her, but he was rich, and a man cannot freely leave a prospering business because his domestic life happens not to be happy.

When a man's mind dwells too much on any one subject, no one can tell just how far he will go. The mind is a delicate instrument, and even the law recognizes that it is easily thrown from its balance. Bodman's friends—for he had friends—claim that his mind was unhinged; but neither his friends nor his enemies suspected the truth of the episode, which turned out to be the most important, as it was the most ominous, event in his life.

Whether John Bodman was sane or insane at the time he made up his mind to murder his wife will never be known, but there was certainly craftiness in the method he devised to make the crime appear the result of an accident. Nevertheless, cunning is often a quality in a mind that has gone wrong.

Mrs Bodman well knew how much her presence afflicted her husband, but her nature was as relentless as his, and her hatred of him was, if possible, more bitter than his hatred of her. Wherever he went she accompanied him, and perhaps the idea of murder would never have occurred to him if she had not been so persistent in forcing her presence upon him at all times and on all occasions. So, when he announced to her that he intended to spend the month of July in Switzerland, she said nothing, but made her preparations for the journey. On this occasion he did not protest, as was usual with him, and so to Switzerland this silent couple departed.

There is an hotel near the mountain tops which stands on a ledge over one of the great glaciers. It is a mile and a half above the level of the sea, and it stands alone, reached by a toilsome road that zigzags up the mountain for six miles. There is a wonderful view of snow-peaks and glaciers from the verandahs of this hotel, and in the neighbourhood are many picturesque walks to points more or less dangerous.

John Bodman knew the hotel well, and in happier days he had been intimately acquainted with the vicinity. Now that the thought of murder arose in his mind, a certain spot two miles distant from this inn continually haunted him. It was a point of view overlooking everything, and its extremity was protected by a low and crumbling wall. He arose one morning at four o'clock, slipped unnoticed out of the hotel, and went to this point, which was locally named the Hanging Outlook. His memory had served him well. It was exactly the spot, he said to himself. The mountain which rose up behind it was wild and precipitous. There were no inhabitants near to overlook the place. The distant hotel was hidden by the shoulder of rock. The mountains on the other side of the valley were too far away to make it possible for any casual tourist or native to see what was going on on the Hanging Outlook. Far down in the valley the only town in view seemed like a collection of little toy houses.

One glance over the crumbling wall at the edge was generally sufficient for a visitor of even the strongest nerves. There was a sheer drop of more than a mile straight down, and at the distant bottom were jagged rocks and stunted trees that looked, in the blue haze, like shrubbery.

'This is the spot,' said the man to himself, 'and tomorrow morning is the time.'

John Bodman had planned his crime as grimly and relentlessly, and as coolly, as ever he had concocted a deal on the Stock Exchange. There was no thought in his mind of mercy for his unconscious victim. His hatred had carried him far.

The next morning after breakfast, he said to his wife: 'I intend to take a walk in the mountains. Do you wish to come with me?'

'Yes,' she answered briefly.

'Very well, then,' he said; 'I shall be ready at nine o'clock.'

'I shall be ready at nine o'clock,' she repeated after him.

At that hour they left the hotel together, to which he was shortly to return alone. They spoke no word to each other on their way to the Hanging Outlook. The path was practically level, skirting the mountains, for the Hanging

Outlook was not much higher above the sea than the hotel.

John Bodman had formed no fixed plan for his procedure when the place was reached. He resolved to be guided by circumstances. Now and then a strange fear arose in his mind that she might cling to him and possibly drag him over the precipice with her. He found himself wondering whether she had any premonition of her fate, and one of his reasons for not speaking was the fear that a tremor in his voice might possibly arouse her suspicions. He resolved that his action should be sharp and sudden, that she might have no chance either to help herself, or to drag him with her. Of her screams in that desolate region he had no fear. No one could reach the spot except from the hotel, and no one that morning had left the house, even for an expedition to the glacier—one of the easiest and most popular trips from the place.

Curiously enough, when they came within the sight of the Hanging Outlook, Mrs Bodman stopped and shuddered. Bodman looked at her through the narrow slits of his veiled eyes, and wondered again if she had any suspicion. No one can tell, when two people walk closely together, what unconscious communication one mind may have with another.

'What is the matter?' he asked gruffly. 'Are you tired?'

'John,' she cried, with a gasp in her voice, calling him by his Christian name for the first time in years, 'don't you think that if you had been kinder to me at first, things might have been different?'

'It seems to me,' he answered, not looking at her, 'that it is rather late in the day for discussing that question.'

'I have much to regret,' she said quaveringly. 'Have you nothing?'

'No,' he answered.

'Very well,' replied his wife, with the usual hardness returning to her voice. 'I was merely giving you a chance. Remember that.'

Her husband looked at her suspiciously.

'What do you mean?' he asked, 'giving me a chance? I want no chance nor anything else from you. A man accepts nothing from one he hates. My feeling towards you is, I imagine, no secret to you. We are tied together, and you have done your best to make the bondage insupportable.'

'Yes,' she answered, with her eyes on the ground, 'we are tied together—we are tied together!'

She repeated these words under her breath as they walked the few remaining steps to the Outlook. Bodman sat down upon the crumbling wall. The woman dropped her alpenstock on the rock, and walked nervously to and fro, clasping and unclasping her hands. Her husband caught his breath as the terrible moment drew near.

'Why do you walk about like a wild animal?' he cried. 'Come here and sit down beside me, and be still.'

She faced him with a light he had never before seen in her eyes—a light of insanity and of hatred.

'I walk like a wild animal,' she said, 'because I am one. You spoke a moment ago of your hatred of me; but you are a man, and your hatred is nothing to mine. Bad as you are, much as you wish to break the bond which ties us together, there are still things which I know you would not stoop to. I know there is no thought of murder in your heart, but there is in mine. I will show you, John Bodman, how much I hate you.'

The man nervously clutched the stone beside him, and gave a guilty start as she mentioned murder.

'Yes,' she continued, 'I have told all my friends in England that I believed you intended to murder me in Switzerland.'

'Good God!' he cried. 'How could you say such a thing?'

'I say it to show how much I hate you—how much I am prepared to give for revenge. I have warned the people at the hotel, and when we left two men followed us. The proprietor tried to persuade me not to accompany you. In a few moments those two men will come in sight of the Outlook. Tell them, if you think they will believe you, that it was an accident.'

The mad woman tore from the front of her dress shreds of lace and scattered them around.

Bodman started up to his feet, crying, 'What are you about?' But before he could move towards her she precipitated herself over the wall, and went shrieking and whirling down the awful abyss.

The next moment two men came hurriedly round the edge of the rock, and found the man standing alone. Even in his bewilderment he realized that if he told the truth he would not be believed.

# The Meeting

### ROBERT SCOTT

'How is it that I send to the market a young man strong and fearless and full of health but he returns shaking like a leaf in the wind?'

'Master, I am afraid.'

'I need no prophet to tell me that.'

'Master, the market was full of jostling women and quarrelling servants but in the corner by the sherbet seller I saw one who glared at me, who pointed and nodded and showed his teeth. Master, it was Death who threatened me.'

'May Allah keep you safe.'

'It is as Allah wills, but, Master, you can help your servant. Lend me your swiftest horse and I will go to my brother in Samarra. Death will not look for me there.'

When his servant had left the merchant went himself to the market-place, where he saw one standing apart by the sherbet seller looking over the crowd.

'May Allah send you long life,' he said.

'It is as Allah wills.'

'This morning my servant came. He says you frowned upon him and threatened him.'

'Your servant is mistaken. I was astonished to see him here, in a Baghdad market-place, when I have a meeting with him tonight in Samarra.'

# The Veldt

## RAY BRADBURY

'George, I wish you'd look at the nursery.'

'What's wrong with it?'

'I don't know.'

'Well, then.'

'I just want you to look at it, that's all, or call a psychologist in to look at it.'

'What would a psychologist want with a nursery?'

'You know very well what he'd want.' His wife paused in the middle of the kitchen and watched the stove busy humming to itself, making supper for four.

'It's just that the nursery is different now than it was.'

'All right, let's have a look.'

They walked down the hall of their soundproofed, Happylife Home, which had cost them thirty thousand dollars installed, this house which clothed and fed and rocked them to sleep and played and sang and was good to them. Their approach sensitized a switch somewhere and the nursery light flicked on when they came within ten feet of it. Similarly, behind them, in the halls, lights

90

went on and off as they left them behind, with a soft automaticity.

'Well,' said George Hadley.

They stood on the thatched floor of the nursery. It was forty feet across by forty feet long and thirty feet high; it had cost half again as much as the rest of the house. 'But nothing's too good for our children,' George had said.

The nursery was silent. It was empty as a jungle glade at hot high noon. The walls were blank and two dimensional. Now, as George and Lydia Hadley stood in the centre of the room, the walls began to purr and recede into crystalline distance, it seemed, and presently an African veldt appeared, in three dimensions; on all sides, in colours reproduced to the final pebble and bit of straw. The ceiling above them became a deep sky with a hot yellow sun.

George Hadley felt the perspiration start on his brow.

'Let's get out of the sun,' he said. 'This is a little too real. But I don't see anything wrong.'

'Wait a moment, you'll see,' said his wife.

Now the hidden odorophonics were beginning to blow a wind of odour at the two people in the middle of the baked veldtland. The hot straw smell of lion grass, the cool green smell of the hidden water hole, the great rusty smell of animals, the smell of dust like a red paprika in the hot air. And now the sounds: the thump of distant antelope feet on grassy sod, the papery rustling of vultures. A shadow passed through the sky. The shadow flickered on George Hadley's upturned, sweating face.

'Filthy creatures,' he heard his wife say.

'The vultures.'

'You see, there are the lions, far over, that way. Now they're on their way to the water hole. They've just been eating,' said Lydia. 'I don't know what.'

'Some animal.' George Hadley put his hand up to shield off the burning light from his squinted eyes. 'A zebra or a baby giraffe, maybe.'

'Are you sure?' His wife sounded peculiarly tense.

'No, it's a little late to be *sure*,' he said, amused. 'Nothing over there I can see but cleaned bone, and the vultures dropping for what's left.'

'Did you hear that scream?' she asked.

'No.'

'About a minute ago?'

'Sorry, no.'

The lions were coming. And again George Hadley was filled with admiration for the mechanical genius who had conceived this room. A miracle of efficiency selling for an absurdly low price. Every home should have one. Oh, occasionally they frightened you with their clinical accuracy, they startled you, gave you a twinge, but most of the time what fun for everyone, not only your own son and daughter, but for yourself when you felt like a quick jaunt to a foreign land, a quick change of scenery. Well, here it was!

And here were the lions now, fifteen feet away, so real, so feverishly and startlingly real that you could feel the prickling fur on your hand, and your mouth was stuffed with the dusty upholstery smell of their heated pelts, and the yellow of them was in your eyes like the yellow of an exquisite French tapestry, the yellows of lions and summer grass, and the sound of the matted lion lungs exhaling on the silent noontide, and the smell of meat from the panting, dripping mouths.

The lions stood looking at George and Lydia Hadley with terrible green-yellow eyes.

'Watch out!' screamed Lydia.

The lions came running at them.

Lydia bolted and ran. Instinctively, George sprang after her. Outside, in the hall, with the door slammed, he was laughing and she was crying, and they both stood appalled at the other's reaction.

'George!'

'Lydia! Oh, my dear poor sweet Lydia!'

'They almost got us!'

'Walls, Lydia, remember; crystal walls, that's all they are. Oh, they look real, I must admit—Africa in your parlour—but it's all dimensional superactionary, supersensitive colour film and mental tape film behind glass screens. It's all odorophonics and sonics, Lydia. Here's my handkerchief.'

'I'm afraid.' She came to him and put her body against him and cried steadily. 'Did you see? Did you *feel*? It's too real.'

'Now, Lydia . . . '

'You've got to tell Wendy and Peter not to read any more on Africa.'

'Of course . . . of course.' He patted her.

'Promise?'

'Sure.'

'And lock the nursery for a few days until I get my nerves settled.'

'You know how difficult Peter is about that. When I punished him a month ago by locking the nursery for even a few hours—the tantrum he threw! And Wendy too. They *live* for the nursery.'

'It's got to be locked, that's all there is to it.'

'All right.' Reluctantly he locked the huge door. 'You've been working too hard. You need a rest.'

'I don't know . . . I don't know,' she said, blowing her nose, sitting down in a chair that immediately began to rock and comfort her. 'Maybe I don't have enough to do. Maybe I have time to think too much. Why don't we shut the whole house off for a few days and take a vacation?'

'You mean you want to fry my eggs for me?'

'Yes.' She nodded.

'And darn my socks?'

'Yes.' A frantic, watery-eyed nodding.

'And sweep the house?'

'Yes, yes . . . oh, yes.'

'But I thought that's why we bought this house, so we wouldn't have to do anything?'

'That's just it. I feel like I don't belong here. The house is wife and mother now and nursemaid. Can I compete with an African veldt? Can I give a bath and scrub the children as efficiently or quickly as the automatic scrub bath can? I can not. And it isn't just me. It's you. You've been awfully nervous lately.'

'I suppose I have been smoking too much.'

'You look as if you didn't know what to do with yourself in this house, either. You smoke a little more every morning and drink a little more every afternoon and need a little more sedative every night. You're beginning to feel unnecessary too.'

'Am I?' He paused and tried to feel into himself to see what was really there.

'Oh, George!' She looked beyond him, at the nursery door. 'Those lions can't get out of there, can they?'

He looked at the door and saw it tremble as if something had jumped against it from the other side.

'Of course not,' he said.

At dinner they ate alone, for Wendy and Peter were at a special plastic carnival across town and had televised home to say they'd be late, to go ahead eating. So George Hadley, bemused, sat watching the dining-room table produce warm dishes of food from its mechanical interior.

'We forgot the ketchup,' he said.

'Sorry,' said a small voice within the table, and ketchup appeared.

As for the nursery, thought George Hadley, it won't hurt for the children to be locked out of it a while. Too much of anything isn't good for anyone. And it was clearly indicated that the children had been spending a little too much time on Africa. That *sun*. He could feel it on his neck, still, like a hot paw. And the *lions*. And the smell of blood. Remarkable how the nursery caught the telepathic emanations of the children's minds and created life to fill their every desire. The children thought lions, and there were lions. The children thought zebra, and there were zebra. Sun—sun. Giraffe—giraffes. Death and death.

That *last*. He chewed tastelessly on the meat that the table had cut for him. Death thoughts. They were awfully young, Wendy and Peter, for death thoughts. Or, no, you were never too young, really. Long before you knew what death was you were wishing it on someone else. When you were two years old you were shooting people with cap pistols.

But this—the long, hot African veldt—the awful death in the jaws of a lion. And repeated again and again.

'Where are you going?'

He didn't answer Lydia. Preoccupied, he let the lights glow softly on ahead of him, extinguish behind him as he padded to the nursery door. He listened against it. Far away, a lion roared.

He unlocked the door and opened it. Just before he stepped inside, he heard a faraway scream. And then another roar from the lions, which subsided quickly.

He stepped into Africa. How many times in the last year had he opened this door and found Wonderland. Alice, the Mock Turtle, or Aladdin and his Magical Lamp, or Jack Pumpkinhead of Oz, or Dr Doolittle, or the cow jumping over a very real-appearing moon—all the delightful contraptions of a make-believe world. How often had he seen Pegasus flying in the sky ceiling, or seen fountains of red fireworks, or heard angel voices singing. But now, this yellow hot Africa, this bake oven with murder in the heat. Perhaps Lydia was right. Perhaps they needed a little vacation from the fantasy which was growing a bit too real for ten-year-old children. It was all right to exercise one's mind with gymnastic fantasies, but when the lively child mind settled on *one* pattern . . . ? It seemed that, at a distance, for the past month, he had heard lions roaring, and smelled their strong odour seeping as far away as his study door. But, being busy, he had paid it no attention.

George Hadley stood on the African grassland alone. The lions looked up from their feeding, watching him. The only flaw to the illusion was the open door through which he could see his wife, far down the dark hall, like a framed picture, eating her dinner abstractedly.

'Go away,' he said to the lions.

They did not go.

He knew the principle of the room exactly. You

sent out your thoughts. Whatever you thought would appear.

'Let's have Aladdin and his lamp,' he snapped.

The veldtland remained; the lions remained.

'Come on, room! I demand Aladdin!' he said.

Nothing happened. The lions mumbled in their baked pelts. 'Aladdin!'

He went back to dinner. 'The fool room's out of order,' he said. 'It won't respond.'

'Or—'

'Or what?'

'Or it *can't* respond,' said Lydia, 'because the children have thought about Africa and lions and killing so many days that the room's in a rut.'

'Could be.'

'Or Peter's set it to remain that way.'

'*Set* it?'

'He may have got into the machinery and fixed something.'

'Peter doesn't know machinery.'

'He's a wise one for ten. That IQ of his—'

'Nevertheless—'

'Hello, Mom. Hello, Dad.'

The Hadleys turned. Wendy and Peter were coming in the front door, cheeks like peppermint candy, eyes like bright blue agate marbles, a smell of ozone on their jumpers from their trip in the helicopter.

'You're just in time for supper,' said both parents.

'We're full of strawberry ice-cream and hot dogs,' said the children, holding hands. 'But we'll sit and watch.'

'Yes, come tell us about the nursery,' said George Hadley.

The brother and sister blinked at him and then at each other. 'Nursery?'

'All about Africa and everything,' said the father with false joviality.

'I don't understand,' said Peter.

'Your mother and I were just travelling through Africa with rod and reel; Tom Swift and his Electric Lion,' said George Hadley.

'There's no Africa in the nursery,' said Peter simply.

'Oh, come now, Peter. We know better.'

'I don't remember any Africa,' said Peter to Wendy. 'Do you?'

'No.'

'Run see and come tell.'

She obeyed.

'Wendy, come back here!' said George Hadley, but she was gone. The house lights followed her like a flock of fireflies. Too late, he realized he had forgotten to lock the nursery door after his last inspection.

'Wendy'll look and come tell us,' said Peter.

'She doesn't have to tell *me*. I've seen it.'

'I'm sure you're mistaken, father.'

'I'm not, Peter. Come along now.'

But Wendy was back. 'It's not Africa,' she said breathlessly.

'We'll see about this,' said George Hadley, and they all walked down the hall together and opened the nursery door.

There was a green, lovely forest, a lovely river, a purple mountain, high voices singing, and Rima, lovely and mysterious, lurking in the trees with colourful flights of butterflies, like animated bouquets, lingering in her long hair. The African veldtland was gone. The lions were gone. Only Rima was here now, singing a song so beautiful that it brought tears to your eyes.

George Hadley looked in at the changed scene. 'Go to bed,' he said to the children.

They opened their mouths.

'You heard me,' he said.

They went off to the air closet, where a wind sucked them like brown leaves up the flue to their slumber rooms.

George Hadley walked through the singing glade and picked up something that lay in the corner near where the lions had been. He walked slowly back to his wife.

'What is that?' she asked.

'An old wallet of mine,' he said.

He showed it to her. The smell of hot grass was on it and the smell of a lion. There were drops of saliva on it, it had been chewed, and there were blood smears on both sides.

He closed the nursery door and locked it, tight.

In the middle of the night he was still awake and he knew his wife was awake. 'Do you think Wendy changed it?' she said at last, in the dark room.

'Of course.'

'Made it from a veldt into a forest and put Rima there instead of lions?'

'Yes.'

'Why?'

'I don't know. But it's staying locked until I find out.'

'How did your wallet get there?'

'I don't know anything,' he said, 'except that I'm beginning to be sorry we bought that room for the children. If children are neurotic at all, a room like that—'

'It's supposed to help them work off their neuroses in a healthful way.'

'I'm starting to wonder.' He stared at the ceiling.

'We've given the children everything they ever wanted. Is this our reward—secrecy, disobedience?'

'Who was it said, "Children are carpets, they should be stepped on occasionally"? We've never lifted a hand. They're insufferable—let's admit it. They come and go when they like; they treat us as if *we* were offspring. They're spoiled and we're spoiled.'

'They've been acting funny ever since you forbade them to take the rocket to New York a few months ago.'

'They're not old enough to do that alone, I explained.'

'Nevertheless, I've noticed they've been decidedly cool towards us since.'

'I think I'll have David McClean come tomorrow morning to have a look at Africa.'

'But it's not Africa now, it's Green Mansions country and Rima.'

'I have a feeling it'll be Africa again before then.'

A moment later they heard the screams.

Two screams. Two people screaming from downstairs. And then a roar of lions.

'Wendy and Peter aren't in their rooms,' said his wife.

He lay in his bed with his beating heart. 'No,' he said. 'They've broken into the nursery.'

'Those screams . . . they sound familiar.'

'Do they?'

'Yes, awfully.'

And although their beds tried very hard, the two adults couldn't be rocked to sleep for another hour. A smell of cats was in the night air.

'Father?' said Peter.

'Yes.'

Peter looked at his shoes. He never looked at his father any more, nor at his mother. 'You aren't going to lock up the nursery for good, are you?'

'That all depends.'

'On what?' snapped Peter.

'On you and your sister. If you intersperse this Africa with a little variety—oh, Sweden perhaps or Denmark or China—'

'I thought we were free to play as we wished.'

'You are, within reasonable bounds.'

'What's wrong with Africa, father?'

'Oh, so now you admit you have been conjuring up Africa, do you?'

'I wouldn't want the nursery locked up,' said Peter coldly. 'Ever.'

'Matter of fact, we're thinking of turning the whole house off for about a month. Live sort of a carefree one-for-all existence.'

'That sounds dreadful! Would I have to tie my own shoes instead of letting the shoe tier do it? And brush my own teeth and comb my hair and give myself a bath?'

'It would be fun for a change, don't you think?'

'No, it would be horrid. I didn't like it when you took out the picture painter last month.'

'That's because I wanted you to learn to paint all by yourself, son.'

'I don't want to do anything but look and listen and smell; what else *is* there to do?'

'All right, go play in Africa.'

'Will you shut off the house sometime soon?'

'We're considering it.'

'I don't think you'd better consider it any more, father.'

'I won't have any threats from my son!'

'Very well.' And Peter strolled off to the nursery.

'Am I on time?' said David McClean.

'Breakfast?' asked George Hadley.

'Thanks, had some. What's the trouble?'

'David, you're a psychologist.'

'I should hope so.'

'Well, then, have a look at our nursery. You saw it a year ago when you dropped by; did you notice anything peculiar about it then?'

'Can't say I did; the usual violences, a tendency towards a slight paranoia here or there, usual in children because they feel persecuted by parents constantly, but, oh, really nothing.'

They walked down the hall. 'I locked the nursery up,' explained the father, 'and the children broke back into it during the night. I let them stay so they could form the patterns for you to see.'

There was a terrible screaming from the nursery.

'There it is,' said George Hadley. 'See what you make of it.'

They walked in on the children without rapping.

The screams had faded. The lions were feeding.

'Run outside a moment, children,' said George Hadley. 'No, don't change the mental combination. Leave the walls as they are. Get!'

With the children gone, the two men stood studying the lions clustered at a distance, eating with great relish whatever it was they had caught.

'I wish I knew what it was,' said George Hadley. 'Sometimes I can almost see. Do you think if I brought high-powered binoculars here and—'

David McClean laughed drily. 'Hardly.' He turned to study all four walls. 'How long has this been going on?'

'A little over a month.'

'It certainly doesn't *feel* good.'

'I want facts, not feelings.'

'My dear George, a psychologist never saw a fact in his life. He only hears about feelings; vague things. This doesn't feel good, I tell you. Trust my hunches and my instincts. I have a nose for something bad. This is very bad. My advice to you is to have the whole damn room torn down and your children brought to me every day during the next year for treatment.'

'Is it that bad?'

'I'm afraid so. One of the original uses of these nurseries was so that we could study the patterns left on the walls by the child's mind, study at our leisure, and help the child. In this case, however, the room has become a channel towards—destructive thoughts, instead of a release away from them.'

'Didn't you sense this before?'

'I sensed only that you had spoiled your children more than most. And now you're letting them down in some way. What way?'

'I wouldn't let them go to New York.'

'What else?'

'I've taken a few machines from the house and threatened them, a month ago, with closing up the nursery unless they did their homework. I did close it for a few days to show I meant business.'

'Ah, ha!'

'Does that mean anything?'

'Everything. Where before they had a Santa Claus now they have a Scrooge. Children prefer Santas. You've let this room and this house replace you and your wife in your children's affections. This room is their mother and father, far more important in their lives than their real parents. And now you come along and want to shut it off. No wonder there's hatred here. You can feel it coming out of the sky. Feel that sun. George, you'll have to change your life. Like too many others, you've built it around creature comforts. Why, you'd starve tomorrow if something went wrong with your kitchen. You wouldn't know how to tap an egg. Nevertheless, turn everything off. Start new. It'll take time. But we'll make good children out of bad in a year, wait and see.'

'But won't the shock be too much for the children, shutting the room up abruptly, for good?'

'I don't want them going any deeper into this, that's all.'

The lions were finished with their red feast.

The lions were standing on the edge of the clearing watching the two men.

'Now *I'm* feeling persecuted,' said McClean. 'Let's get out of here. I never have cared for these damned rooms. Make me nervous.'

'The lions look real, don't they?' said George Hadley. 'I don't suppose there's any way—'

'What?'

'—that they could *become* real?'

'Not that I know.'

'Some flaw in the machinery, a tampering or something?'

'No.'

They went to the door.

'I don't imagine the room will like being turned off,' said the father.

'Nothing ever likes to die—even a room.'

'I wonder if it hates me for wanting to switch it off?'

'Paranoia is thick around here today,' said David McClean. 'You can follow it like a spoor. Hello.' He bent and picked up a bloody scarf. 'This yours?'

'No.' George Hadley's face was rigid. 'It belongs to Lydia.'

They went to the fuse box together and threw the switch that killed the nursery.

The two children were in hysterics. They screamed and pranced and threw things. They yelled and sobbed and swore and jumped at the furniture.

'You can't do that to the nursery, you can't!'

'Now, children.'

The children flung themselves on to a couch, weeping.

'George,' said Lydia Hadley, 'turn on the nursery, just for a few moments. You can't be so abrupt.'

'No.'

'You can't be so cruel.'

'Lydia, it's off, and it stays off. And the whole damn house dies as of here and now. The more I see of the mess we've put ourselves in, the more it sickens me. We've been contemplating our mechanical, electronic navels for too long. My God, how we need a breath of honest air!'

And he marched about the house turning off the voice clocks, the stoves, the heaters, the shoe shiners, the shoe lacers, the body scrubbers and swabbers and massagers, and every other machine he could put his hand to.

The house was full of dead bodies, it seemed. It felt like a mechanical cemetery. So silent. None of the humming hidden energy of machines waiting to function at the tap of a button.

'Don't let them do it!' wailed Peter at the ceiling, as if he was talking to the house, the nursery. 'Don't let father kill everything.' He turned to his father. 'Oh, I hate you!'

'Insults won't get you anywhere.'

'I wish you were dead!'

'We were, for a long while. Now we're going to really start living. Instead of being handled and massaged, we're going to *live*.'

Wendy was still crying and Peter joined her again. 'Just a moment, just one moment, just another moment of nursery,' they wailed.

'Oh, George,' said his wife, 'it can't hurt.'

'All right . . . all right, if they'll only just shut up. One minute, mind you, and then off forever.'

'Daddy, Daddy, Daddy!' sang the children, smiling with wet faces.

'And then we're going on a vacation. David McClean is coming back in half an hour to help us move out and get to the airport. I'm going to dress. You turn the nursery on for a minute, Lydia, just a minute, mind you.'

And the three of them went babbling off while he let himself be vacuumed upstairs through the air flue and set about dressing himself. A minute later Lydia appeared.

'I'll be glad when we get away,' she sighed.

'Did you leave them in the nursery?'

'I wanted to dress too. Oh, that horrid Africa. What can they see in it?'

'Well, in five minutes we'll be on our way to Iowa. Lord, how did we ever get in this house? What prompted us to buy a nightmare?'

'Pride, money, foolishness.'

'I think we'd better get downstairs before those kids get engrossed with those damned beasts again.'

Just then they heard the children calling, 'Daddy, Mommy, come quick . . . quick!'

They went downstairs in the air flue and ran down the hall. The children were nowhere in sight. 'Wendy? Peter!'

They ran into the nursery. The veldtland was empty save for the lions waiting, looking at them. 'Peter, Wendy?'

The door slammed.

'Wendy, Peter!'

George Hadley and his wife whirled and ran back to the door.

'Open the door!' cried George Hadley, trying the knob. 'Why, they've locked it from the outside! Peter!' He beat at the door. 'Open up!'

He heard Peter's voice outside, against the door.

'Don't let them switch off the nursery and the house,' he was saying.

Mr and Mrs George Hadley beat at the door. 'Now, don't be ridiculous, children. It's time to go. Mr McClean'll be here in a minute and . . . '

And then they heard the sounds.

The lions on three sides of them, in the yellow veldt grass, padding through the dry straw, rumbling and roaring in their throats.

The lions.

Mr Hadley looked at his wife and they turned and looked back at the beasts edging slowly forward, crouching, tails stiff.

Mr and Mrs Hadley screamed.

And suddenly they realized why those other screams had sounded familiar.

'Well, here I am,' said David McClean in the nursery doorway. 'Oh, hello.' He stared at the two children seated in the centre of the open glade eating a little picnic lunch. Beyond them was the water hole and the yellow veldtland; above was the hot sun. He began to perspire. 'Where are your father and mother?'

The children looked up and smiled. 'Oh, they'll be here directly.'

'Good, we must get going.' At a distance Mr McClean saw the lions fighting and clawing and then quieting down to feed in silence under the shady trees.

He squinted at the lions with his hand up to his eyes.

Now the lions were done feeding. They moved to the water hole to drink.

A shadow flickered over Mr McClean's hot face. Many shadows flickered. The vultures were dropping down the blazing sky.

'A cup of tea?' asked Wendy in the silence.

# Death's Murderers

## GERALDINE McCAUGHREAN

The man Grab was slumped over a table at the Tabard Inn in Southwark—(you may know the place). He had wetted his brain in beer, and it weighed heavy. The clanging of the church bell registered dully in his ears. 'Who are they burying?' he asked.

Old Harry, the landlord, who was wiping tables close by, said, 'Don't you know? I wondered why you weren't at the funeral—him being a friend of yours. It's Colley the Fence. Caught it last Wednesday and gone today. Him and his wife and his two boys.'

'Caught what?' demanded Grab, grasping Harry's arm.

'The Black Death, of course!'

Then another customer chimed in. 'Ay, they do say the Plague came to Combleton over yonder, and Death laid hands on every man, woman, and child and carried 'em off.'

'Where? Carried them off where?' demanded Grab, fighting his way through drink-haze like a ghost through cobwebs.

109

'Who knows where Death carries men off to,' said a deeply hooded character sitting in the corner of the bar, 'but he sure enough comes for every man in the end. And he's taken twice his share recently, thanks to the Plague.'

Tears of indignation started into Grab's eyes. 'I don't see what gives Death the right to go carrying off anyone!' he slurred. 'And if you ask me, it's about time some brave soul stood up to Death and put an end to his carryings-on—his carryings-off I mean. Dip! Cut! Where are you?' And he stumbled off into the sunlight to look for his two closest friends.

Dip was at home in bed, but not for long. Grab knocked him up and called him into the street. They met with Cut coming home from a card-game and cursing his empty pockets.

Grab threw an arm over each friend's shoulder. 'Have you heard? Old Colley the Fence is dead. Death carried off him and all his family in a couple of days. Let's take an oath, friends, not to rest until we've tracked down this "Death" fellow and stuck a knife between his ribs. Think what the mayor and parish would pay if we brought in Death's dead body. Besides—how many purses do you think he's emptied on the dark highway, eh? Death must have made himself quite a walletful by now.'

Cut fingered his sharp penknife—the one he used for cutting purses. Dip felt his fingers itch at the promise of rich pickings. 'We're with you, neighbour Grab!' they cried, and off they reeled, not the sum total of one brain between the three of them.

They looked for Death in the graveyard, but decided he must be out hunting the living instead. They looked for Death in the fields, but he had always gone before they arrived, leaving the flowers doomed to wither and the leaves, sooner or later, to fall.

Then, as the daylight failed, they saw a small figure on the road ahead. 'We've caught him up!' cried Grab, and they fell on the man, with flailing fists.

'Wait a minute! This isn't Death at all!' said Cut, letting his penknife fall. 'He's just some silly old duffer. Look at him—he's older than Methuselah!'

The old man peered at them out of the dark recesses of his hood. His face was as white and bony as a skull, with purse-string lips and eyes sunk deep in red whorls of wrinkled skin. His hands were as brown as vinegar-paper, and his back hunched over like a turtle's shell. 'What do you want with me? Don't I have enough to put up with? Can't you leave a poor blighted old creature in peace?'

'You're no good to us!' Dip said in disgust. 'We wanted Death, not some wrinkled old prune on legs!'

A bitter laugh creaked out through the creature's gappy ribs. '*You* want Death! Ah, not half as much as I do! I'm the one poor beast alive that Death can't carry off. I'm condemned to live for ever and to creep about the Earth in this worn-out old body, getting older and older and older. As for Death—I've just left him under that oak tree yonder. If you hurry, you'll find him still there.'

Cut's knife was raised again. 'So! You've had dealings with him. We'll kill you anyway!'

The fossil of a man let go a sigh that seemed to break through his brittle skin. 'Aaah, I wish you could rob me of this tedious burden, Life. You should pity me, even if you have no respect for my old age. But don't bother to batter on this prison my soul calls a body: you can't free me from it.' He shuffled out from under their raised

111

blades, muttering, 'You're the lucky ones—you might die today!'

'Get to bed with the maggots and mould, you old relic of the Devil,' Grab cursed. 'We're on our way to kill Death. Then no one will have to die any more!' As soon as the old man was out of sight, the three accomplices forgot him completely.

Under the oak tree, there was no sign of Death. But there was a pot of money as big as any crock of gold at the rainbow's end.

Cut tipped the jar over with his foot, and the wealth of seven lifetimes spilled out on to the grass. They looked around. No one was even in sight. And there had been no attempt to hide the gold. It lay there, just inviting them to keep it. Grab and Dip and Cut were suddenly rich!

'Rich! We're rich, rich, rich!' As the gold coins spilled out of the jar, so all thought of their plot to kill Death dropped out of their minds.

'Dip, your legs are youngest,' said Grab. 'Run into town and fetch us some wine. We've got to celebrate luck like this!'

'Why is it always me?' Dip threw a sulky look at the gold, but was given only one coin to buy the makings of a party.

'We'll both stay and guard it, don't you worry,' Grab assured him. 'Be quick, lad. When you get back we'll decide what we're to do with it all—what mansions we'll build, who to bribe, what monks we'll pay to have done in. We don't have to do our own dirty work from now on, boy! We'll be the Three Kings of the Thieves.'

Full of such thoughts, Dip set off into the dusk to buy cakes and wine. The sun was behind him, and his shadow stretched long and spidery ahead, so that he was all the time stepping into his own darkness.

Grab and Cut watched him go, then sat down on either side of the pot of gold. They counted the coins. Somehow it always came to a different number: 848 or 916 or 772. Grab scowled. 'Of course you realize we can't divide it three ways.'

'We can't?'

'You take my word for it. It won't share out evenly.'

'It won't?'

'Two ways, yes. Not three. One of us will have to take less.'

'Oh!'

Cut decided at once that since Dip was the youngest, he should take the smallest share. They both nodded to themselves and settled back to counting the gold. This time there seemed to be 999—or 783, or perhaps 870. But it did not change their opinion that Dip should have less.

'Of course it won't go far between the *three* of us,' Grab mused. 'Not with the cost of living how it is. And you know how Dip squanders money.'

'No?'

'He'll soon have spent all his, and he'll be asking to borrow from us.'

'But I can't spare any of mine!' said Cut anxiously.

'No more can I. There's little enough to share out between two, let alone three.' They lapsed into silence, and above them the oak's heavy branches groaned while the gold coins clinked between their fingers. 'Supposing . . .' said Cut, 'just supposing Dip was to meet with an accident on his way back from town . . .'

'So many thieves these days . . .' said Grab nodding sadly. 'So many ruffians and murderers.'

Meanwhile, Dip was watching his shadow move ahead of him on the roadway like a black plough. How big it was—much bigger than him. When he had his share of the money, he would be a bigger man in every way. No more creeping through the crowds at fairs, cutting purses and catching the pennies that dropped. He could walk tall and stately, in fur-trimmed robes, and people would touch their forelocks and step aside. Beggars would fight for the chance to plead with him. And if he felt like it, he could drive them away with a pelting of money, and see them grovel in his wake.

Ah, but if he was going to start giving money away, there would be less for the true necessities—drink and women and gambling. In fact he could think of so many good uses for the gold that it seemed a pity Cut and Grab had been with him when he had found the jar. Really, the more he thought about it, the less fair it seemed that they had bunked in on his good fortune.

As he reached the outskirts of the town, he noticed an apothecary's sign hanging over a door. He did not remember ever having seen it before, but he knocked without hesitation.

'What's your trouble, young man, that you rouse me from my bed?' An ancient, hairless head poked out of an upstairs window, grotesque and vaguely familiar with its parchment-yellow shine. 'Rats,' said Dip, his head muffled up in his cloak. 'The rats are eating me out of house and home.'

'Here. One drop of this will finish them off. Have it for free.' The ancient apothecary must have had the poison in his pocket, for he dropped it down at once, into Dip's outstretched hands. 'It couldn't be simpler,' he called as

114

the boy hurried off to the inn. Dip bought three bottles of wine. Every last drop of the poison went into two of the bottles. The third he marked carefully to be sure of telling it apart. Then he was off to collect his rightful share of the golden hoard—every last coin of it.

In the pitch dark of late evening, he stumbled over Cut and Grab snoozing under the oak tree in the deep grass. 'Thought you'd forgotten us,' said Grab with a sort of grin.

'I wouldn't forget my two old friends, now would I?' Dip opened his bottle of wine and took a swig. 'Have a drink, why don't you?' Cut and Grab knelt up and groped for the wine, their hands brushing Dip's face in the dark. They moved to either side of their good friend . . .

Along the road came the sudden noise of the plague cart rattling out of the town towards the lime pits in Ring-a-Rosey Hollow. They all three watched its creaking progress beneath the light of the coachmen's torches. Its white cargo of dead bodies joggled against one another like restless sleepers. A limp arm dangling through the cart rails swung to and fro, for all the world as if it were beckoning them . . .

'We took an oath to kill old Death,' said Cut, remembering.

'We'll get round to it some time,' said Grab, drawing his dagger. 'One thing at a time.'

He plunged the knife into the back of Dip's neck. It met with the seam of his hood, and the lad looked round in astonishment in time to make out the shape of Cut, outlined against the moon. Then Cut's sharp penknife caught him under the ribs and he sprawled, cursing, to his death, among the gnarled roots of the oak tree.

'It's done,' Grab panted, and his throat felt suddenly

dry. 'Let's drink to our partnership, Cut. Where did he put the bottles?'

By feeling along the ground, they found the three bottles in the long grass. The opened one had emptied itself into the ground, but the others were intact. A bottle a-piece, Cut and Grab sat with their backs to the oak tree, and drank to their new-found fortune.

In the morning, Death came back for his pot of gold. He wrapped it in the miserable rags of his decaying cloak, close to his gappy ribs. The three corpses under the tree made no move to stop him, and he left them to a wealth of flies and crows before continuing his endless journey. The gold weighed light in his arms. Though his bones were dry and his muscles were like the withered tendrils of a grapeless vine, his strength was immense. He could carry off the biggest or strongest of men—even though, like any man or beast, he could never carry off himself.

# A Hundred Steps

### ROBERT SCOTT

John paused in his descent, hand against the worn stone wall, and smiled grimly. It had been their first quarrel. No, not quarrel. Difference. Their first difference.

'A hundred steps to heaven or a thousand steps to hell,' the old woman had said if he understood her correctly. So he had insisted on driving out to the tower even though Janet complained bitterly that climbing derelict old towers wasn't her idea of heaven, especially on the last day of their honeymoon.

'Loosen up,' he had said. 'It'll only take half an hour and we'll get a marvellous view from the top. Then we can drive on to the coast.'

'It'll be too late.'

'A hundred steps to the top,' he had reminded her. 'That's what the old woman said. A hundred steps for lovers to see their heaven.' He was sure she had said '*their* heaven'.

'I'll wait here,' she insisted, smiling brightly and

117

opening her copy of *True Romances*. And she stayed in the car, shoes off, feet tucked under her.

There had been no view of heaven from the top, only a thick, blanketing mist. And now? Well, now . . . He drew a deep breath, refusing to let his brain admit the terror that was ready to overwhelm him. A hundred steps to heaven or a thousand steps to hell. He had counted the steps on his way up and now he was counting them again on the way down.

'Nine hundred and eighty-two,' he muttered. 'Nine hundred and eighty-three. Nine hundred and . . .'

# The Cathedral Crypt

### JOHN WYNDHAM

'The past seems so close here,' Clarissa said, as though she thought aloud. 'Somehow it hasn't been allowed to fade into dead history.'

Raymond nodded. He did not speak, but she could see that he understood and that he, like herself, felt the weight of antiquity pressing down upon this Spanish city. Half unconsciously she elaborated:

'Most of our cities strive for change, they throw away the past for the sake of progress. And there are a few, like Rome, truly eternal cities which sail majestically on, absorbing change as it comes. But I don't feel that this city is quite like that. Here, the past seems . . . seems arrogant, as if it were fighting against the present. It is determined to conquer all the new forces. Look at that, for instance.'

A car, new and glossy, was standing before the cathedral door. A priest blessed it with upraised hand while he murmured prayers for the safety of the travellers.

'Commending it to the care of God, and the charge of

119

St Christopher,' Raymond remarked. 'At home they say that the cars empty the churches; here they even bring the car to church. You're right, my dear, the past is not going to give in here without a battle.'

The car, with its celestial premium paid, drove on its way, and with it went all sign of the twentieth century. Late sunlight poured upon a scene entirely medieval. It flooded the cathedral's western face, turning it from grey to palest rose, showing it as something which was more than stone upon stone, a thing which lived though it rested eternally. The fragile beauty of living things was built into those Gothic spears which sped heavenward. Such traceries and filigrees, such magnificent aspiration could not absorb men's art and lives, and yet remain mere stone. Something of the builders' souls was swept up to live for ever among the clustered pinnacles.

'It's very, very lovely,' Clarissa whispered. 'It makes me feel small—and rather frightened.'

Over the dark doorways a row of stone saints in their niches stretched across the façade. Above them a rose window stared like a Cyclops' unblinking eye. Higher still, gargoyles leered sunward, keeping their ceaseless watch for devils. The cathedral was a fantasy of faith; spirit had helped to build it no less than hands: a dream in stone on a foundation of souls.

'Yes—that is beauty,' Raymond said.

He stepped towards the open doors. Clarissa, on his arm, hung back a little, she did not know why. Beauty can awe, but can it alone send a deeper prick of fear?

'We are going inside?' she asked.

Her husband caught the tone of her voice; he looked at her with a tinge of surprise. He would obey any wish of hers willingly. The world held nothing dearer than

Clarissa; she had become even more precious in the three weeks since their marriage.

'You'd rather not? You're tired?'

Clarissa shook away her vague fears; they were a foolishness unworthy of her. Besides, Raymond obviously wanted to go in.

'No. Of course we must look at it. They say the inside is even more beautiful than the outside,' she agreed.

But as they walked about the huge, darkening place her uneasiness came creeping back. Ethereal fears clustered within and around her, clinging but impalpable. She fastened to Raymond and his firm reality, trying to share his pleasure in the pictures, shrines, and sculptures. Together they gazed up at the huge, shining crucifix slung from the distant roof, but her mind did not follow his words as he admired it. She was thinking how quiet, how lonely it was in this great place. Here and there one or two dim figures moved silently as ghosts, points of light shone in far, dark corners like stars in the blackness of space. There was a sense of peace, but not the peace of tranquillity . . .

They crossed to the side chapels where Raymond took a lengthy interest in the decorations and furnishing. Some time had passed before he looked up and noticed his wife's pallor.

'What is it? You're not ill, darling?'

'No,' she assured him. 'No, I'm quite all right.'

It was the truth. There was nothing wrong with her save only an overwhelming desire to get back to the familiarities of noises and people.

'Anyhow, we had better go. They'll be wanting to close the place soon,' Raymond said. They returned to the central aisle and turned towards the entrance. Now that the sun had set the western end was very dim. The lights were few and feeble, pale candles and a lamp or two; the rose window was no more than a blur; the shape of the doorway, invisible. With misgiving, Raymond hastened his steps. Clarissa clutched his arm more tightly.

'Surely they haven't—' he began, but he left the sentence unfinished as they both saw that the heavy doors were shut.

'They must have overlooked us when we were in that chapel,' he said with more cheerfulness than he felt. 'I'll try knocking.'

But the pounding of his fists against the massive doors was childishly futile. Sledgehammer blows could scarcely have been heard through those solid timbers. Together they shouted. Their voices fled away through the empty arches. The sound, flung from wall to wall, returned to them, a distorted, eerie travesty.

'Don't,' implored Clarissa, 'don't shout any more—it frightens me.'

Raymond stopped at once, but he did not admit in words that he too had felt fearful of the echoes, as though he were disturbing things which should be left to sleep.

'Perhaps there is a smaller door open somewhere,' he suggested, but with little hope in his tones.

Their heels clicked sharply on the flagstones as they searched. Clarissa fought down an absurd impulse to walk on tiptoe. Each door they tried seemed equipped with a more loudly clattering latch and more raucously grinding bolts than the last. A few opened, but none of these led into the open.

'Locked,' said Raymond disgustedly as they reached the main door once more. 'Every single entrance locked.

I'm afraid we're prisoners.' Half-heartedly he hammered again on the wood.

'But we can't stay here.'

There was a piteous sound in Clarissa's voice, like a child imploring not to be left in the dark. He put his arm round her and she pressed thankfully closer.

'We must. There's no help for it. After all, it might be worse. We're together and we're perfectly safe.'

'Yes, but—oh, I suppose it's silly to be afraid.'

'There's nothing to be afraid of, darling. We can go back into that little chapel and make ourselves as comfortable as we can in there so that we'll forget that all this outer part exists. There are cushions on the benches, and we can use hassocks for pillows. Oh, we might be far worse off.'

Raymond woke suddenly at the slight movement of Clarissa in his arms.

'What is it?' he mumbled sleepily.

'Sh—Listen!' she told him.

She watched his face as he obeyed, part fearful lest he should not hear the sound, but in greater part hoping that he would prove it an hallucination. He sat upright.

'Yes, I can hear it. What on earth—?' He glanced at his watch; it showed half-past one. 'What can they be doing at this time?'

They listened in silence for some moments. The confused sound down by the entrance clarified into a chant of massive solemnity. No words could reach them, only harmony rising and falling like the surge of long, slow waves.

Raymond half rose. Clarissa seized his arm, her voice imploring:

'No . . . no, you mustn't, it's—' She stopped, at a loss. There was no word to express her sensation. But it touched him, too, like a warning. He relaxed and dropped back to the seat.

The voices approached slowly. The chant rolled on. Occasionally it would rise from its ululation to a paean and then sink back again to its woeful monotony.

The two in the chapel crept forward until only one high-backed bench hid them from the nave. There they crouched, peering out into the dimness.

The slow procession passed. First the acolytes with swinging censers, behind them a cross bearer, then a single, robed figure leading a dozen brown-habited monks, chanting, their faces uncertainly lit by the candles they carried. Then the Sisters of some black-robed Order, their faces gleaming, white as paper out of their sombreness. Two more monks, holding by ropes a lonely nun . . .

She was young, not ageless like the rest, but the beauty of her face was submerged in anguish. Bright tears of fear and misery poured from her wide eyes, trickling down upon her clothes. She could not brush them away nor hide her face, for her arms were tightly bound behind her back. Now and then her voice rose in a frightened call above the chanting. A weak, thin cry which choked in a tightened throat. She darted glances right and left, twisted to look behind her in hopeless desperation. Twice she hung back, writhing her arms in their cords. The two monks before her pulled on the ropes, dragging her forward. Once she fell to her knees and with lips moving, gazed up at the immense cross in the roof. She implored mercy and forgiveness, but the tugging ropes forced her on.

Clarissa turned horrified eyes to her husband. She saw

that he also had understood and knew the rite which was to follow. He murmured something too low for her to catch.

The deliberate procession with its spangle of candles approached the altar. Each row genuflected before it turned away to the left. Despair seemed to snap the last stay of hope in the nun as she passed it, drooping. Raymond leaned further out of the chapel to watch the file disappear into a small doorway. Then he returned to his wife and took her hand. Neither spoke.

Clarissa was too deeply shocked for speech. A nun who had broken her vows—she knew the old punishment for that. They would put her—she shuddered and clutched Raymond's hand the tighter. They couldn't . . . they couldn't do that! Not now. Centuries ago, perhaps, but not today. But the thought of her own words came back to her: 'The past seems so close here,' she had said. She shuddered again.

Sounds stole out of the little door into the cathedral.

A short, weak scuffle; something between a gasp and a whimper; a voice which spoke in heavy, sonorous tones:

*'In nomine patris, et filii, et spiritus sancti—'*

A muffled clash. The ring of the trowel on the stone. Clarissa fainted.

'They're gone,' Raymond was saying. 'Come quickly!'

'What—?' Clarissa was still uncertain, bemused.

'Come along. We may be in time to save her yet. There must be a little air in there.'

He was pulling Clarissa by the wrist, dragging her after him, out of the chapel, towards the small door.

'But if they should come back—?'

'They've gone, I tell you. I heard them bolt the big doors.'

'But—' Clarissa was terrified. If the monks found out that there had been witnesses . . . What then?

'Hurry or we'll be too late.'

Raymond seized a candle from its altar and pulled at the small door. For its size it was heavy, and swung back slowly. He ran down the curving flight of stone steps beyond, Clarissa at his heels. The crypt below was small. One candle sufficed to show all there was to see. The two side walls were smooth, it was the one opposite at which they stared. It showed the shape of two niches long filled in, three more niches, empty and darkly waiting, and one lighter patch of new stones and white mortar.

Raymond set down his candle and ran to the recent work, one hand fumbling for a knife in his pocket. Clarissa raked at the damp mortar with her finger nails.

'Just enough to let us get a hold on this stone,' he muttered as he scraped.

He clenched his strong fingers on its edges. At his first heave it loosened, a second pull, and it fell with a thud at his feet.

But there was another sound in the crypt. They whirled round to stare into the expressionless faces of six monks.

In the morning, only one niche stood empty and darkly waiting.

# The Ghost of the Blue Chamber

### JEROME K. JEROME

'I don't want to make you fellows nervous,' began my uncle in a peculiarly impressive, not to say blood-curdling, tone of voice, 'and if you would rather that I did not mention it, I won't; but, as a matter of fact, this very house, in which we are now sitting, is haunted.'

'You don't say that!' exclaimed Mr Coombes.

'What's the use of your saying I don't say it when I have just said it?' retorted my uncle somewhat pettishly. 'You do talk so foolishly. I tell you the house is haunted. Regularly on Christmas Eve the Blue Chamber [they called the room next to the nursery the 'blue chamber', at my uncle's, most of the toilet service being of that shade] is haunted by the ghost of a sinful man—a man who once killed a Christmas wait with a lump of coal.'

'How did he do it?' asked Mr Coombes, with eager anxiousness. 'Was it difficult?'

'I do not know how he did it,' replied my uncle; 'he did not explain the process. The wait had taken up a position just inside the front gate, and was singing a ballad. It is presumed that, when he opened his mouth for B flat, the lump of coal was thrown by the sinful man from one of the windows, and that it went down the wait's throat and choked him.'

'You want to be a good shot, but it is certainly worth trying,' murmured Mr Coombes thoughtfully.

'But that was not his only crime, alas!' added my uncle 'Prior to that he had killed a solo cornet player.'

'No! Is that really a fact?' exclaimed Mr Coombes.

'Of course it's a fact,' answered my uncle testily; 'at all events, as much a fact as you can expect to get in a case of this sort.

'How very captious you are this evening. The circumstantial evidence was overwhelming. The poor fellow, the cornet player, had been in the neighbourhood barely a month. Old Mr Bishop, who kept the "Jolly Sand Boys" at the time, and from whom I had the story, said he had never known a more hard-working and energetic solo cornet player. He, the cornet player, only knew two tunes, but Mr Bishop said that the man could not have played with more vigour, or for more hours a day, if he had known forty. The two tunes he did play were "Annie Laurie" and "Home, Sweet Home"; and as regards his performance of the former melody, Mr Bishop said that a mere child could have told what it was meant for.

'This musician—this poor, friendless artist used to come regularly and play in this street just opposite for two hours every evening. One evening he was seen, evidently in response to an invitation, going into this very house, *but was never seen coming out of it!*'

'Did the townsfolk try offering any reward for his recovery?' asked Mr Coombes.

'Not a ha'penny,' replied my uncle.

'Another summer,' continued my uncle, 'a German band visited here, intending—so they announced on their arrival—to stay till the autumn.

'On the second day from their arrival, the whole company, as fine and healthy a body of men as one could wish to see, were invited to dinner by this sinful man, and, after spending the whole of the next twenty-four hours in bed, left the town a broken and dyspeptic crew; the parish doctor, who had attended them, giving it as his opinion that it was doubtful if they would, any of them, be fit to play an air again.'

'You—you don't know the recipe, do you?' asked Mr Coombes.

'Unfortunately I do not,' replied my uncle; 'but the chief ingredient was said to have been railway refreshment-room pork pie.

'I forget the man's other crimes,' my uncle went on; 'I used to know them all at one time, but my memory is not what it was. I do not, however, believe I am doing his memory an injustice in believing that he was not entirely unconnected with the death, and subsequent burial, of a gentleman who used to play the harp with his toes; and that neither was he altogether unresponsible for the lonely grave of an unknown stranger who had once visited the neighbourhood, an Italian peasant lad, a performer upon the barrel organ.

'Every Christmas Eve,' said my uncle, cleaving with low impressive tones the strange awed silence that, like a shadow, seemed to have slowly stolen into and settled down upon the room, 'the ghost of this sinful man haunts

the Blue Chamber, in this very house. There, from
midnight until cock-crow, amid wild muffled shrieks and
groans and mocking laughter and the ghostly sound of
horrid blows, it does fierce phantom fight with the spirits
of the solo cornet player and the murdered wait, assisted
at intervals by the shades of the German band; while the
ghost of the strangled harpist plays mad ghostly melodies
with ghostly toes on the ghost of a broken harp.'

# The Skeleton in the Closet

RICHARD AND JUDY DOCKREY YOUNG

One day some new kids at school were helping the janitor clean up down in the basement where the huge steam heating system was located. They went further back into the dark recesses of the basement and found a dusty door that looked like it hadn't been opened in years.

They took hold of the doorknob, which almost fell off in their hands. They pulled, but the door was stuck because the hinges had gotten rusty.

Finally, they pulled really hard and the door swung open. Dust poured out in a cloud. When the dust cleared, the kids saw a horrible sight.

There, slumped over against the wall, was a rotten skeleton.

They called the janitor, who called the police.

For a long time no one could figure out who the skeleton had been. Then, finally, they were able to identify the rotten tennis shoes, and knew who it was.

It was the 1954 school hide-and-seek champion.

# *One Chance*

### ETHEL HELENE COEN

It was the terrible summer of 1720. The plague hung darkly over shuddering New Orleans. Its black wings beat at every door, and there were few that had not opened to its dread presence. Paul had seen his mother, father, sisters, and friends swept down by its mowing sickle. Only Marie remained for him—beautiful Marie with her love for him that he knew was stronger than any plague—the one thing in all the world that was left to sustain him.

'Let us fly from this accursed place,' he pleaded. 'Let us try to find happiness elsewhere. Neither of us has a tie to bind us here—is not your sister to be buried this very day? Ah, Saint Louis has seen many such scenes in this last month—we will fly to Canada and begin all over.'

'But, my darling,' she protested, 'you forget the quarantine: no one is allowed to enter or leave the city; your plan is hopeless.'

'No . . . no . . . I have a plan—such a terrible one that I shudder to think of it. Here it is—'

While he rapidly sketched their one desperate chance Marie's face blanched, but when he finished, she agreed.

The daughter of the mayor had died that morning. A special dispensation had been secured to ship her body to Charleston for burial. The body rested in its casket in Saint Louis cathedral and was to be shipped by boat that night.

At six o'clock that evening the cathedral was empty save for its silent occupants awaiting burial. The tall wax tapers glimmered fitfully over the scene of desolation. Paul and Marie crept in and went to the casket of the mayor's daughter. Paul rapidly unscrewed the wooden top, removed the slight body, put it into a large sack; and Marie, nearly swooning from terror, got into the coffin.

'Here is a flask of water,' Paul whispered, 'and remember—not a sound, no matter what happens. I shall sneak aboard the boat before it sails at nine. After we are out for half an hour I will let you out of this. It is our only chance.'

'Yes, I know,' Marie whispered chokingly. 'I shall make no sound . . . now go . . . the priests will soon be back, so one last kiss, until we are on the boat.'

He kissed her passionately, then loosely screwed the top on the casket.

Stealing with his awful burden to the yard in the back of the cathedral he remembered a deep, dried-up well in one corner of the yard. Just the place to dispose of the body.

God rest the poor girl's soul, he thought; she, wherever she is, will understand that I meant no sacrilege to her remains, but this is my one chance of happiness . . . my only chance.

His task ended, he climbed the iron wall and walked rapidly up Pirates Alley and wandered over the Vieux

Carré until eight-thirty. Thank God—it was time to try
the success of their daring venture. His head whirled and
his heart beat like a trip-hammer as he slipped on to the
boat unobserved by any but the dock hands, who probably
considered him one of their number. He secreted himself
in a dark corner and waited. After centuries had passed,
or so it seemed to him, the boat started moving. It would
not be long now. He did not stop to think what would
happen when they were caught—that would take care of
itself.

Ah—voices, coming nearer and nearer. From his
corner Paul could distinctly see the silhouettes of the two
men who were approaching.

'Yes,' said one, 'it is sad. The mayor is broken-
hearted—we were going to take her body to Charleston—
but the mayor had her buried from Saint Louis just after
the sun went down.'

# Every Litter Bit Hurts

## MICHAEL AVALLONE

The Impala gleamed shiny and red on the sloping driveway. Bobby ran towards it, eyes twinkling, clapping his hands. He and Daddy were going for a ride! He paused, a bit puzzled, while his father lifted the hood and studied the engine carefully, peering at the electrical terminals of the starter to be sure no new wires had been added, wires which could connect to a dynamite bomb.

Jamison hadn't been that careful, and Jamison had been killed.

Bobby, of course, had no way of knowing the reason for his father's action, nor did the thought remain with him long. All he knew was that he and his father were going for a ride! And Daddy had strapped on his gun, even. Right under his coat in that dark leather holster.

The large man closed the hood, satisfied with his inspection, smiling at the boy.

'Remember,' Daddy was saying, 'don't ever throw anything out of the car. Understood? It's not nice.

Especially when Daddy's driving fast on the highway. It just isn't *nice*, Bobby. You could hit another Daddy in the eye and cause an accident. *Do you understand?*'

Bobby nodded, tugging at the big Impala door.

'Good boy. I knew you'd understand once you knew the reason. Mommy will be proud of you when I tell her.'

Bobby smiled. The words were running around in his head like happy puppies. *Mommy. Proud. Good boy.* When you are only five years of age, those words are glowing beacons of progress and love.

But above all, progress. The march forward, the long trip towards that mysterious land of Growing Up.

'Where are we going today, Daddy? Police station again?' When Daddy took his gun, it almost always meant the police station.

'Daddy's got to go to Elmira,' Robert Black, Sr. said, a funny glint in his eye. 'Part of the job, too. I have to go to the District Attorney to hand over some papers. You know. I told you. We'll meet Mommy there and then maybe we'll take in a movie. Would you like that?'

He paused, lighting a cigarette from the dashboard lighter. Bobby watched him, bursting with ride-fever and pride. He liked the sure look of the strong hands, the keen profile of his father. Sharp, like the face on a coin, under a porkpie hat. Daddy had told him that once and he had remembered. What a funny name for a hat! Maybe Porky the Pig wore porkpie hats, too.

'Mommy's in town?' Bobby prodded with that unswerving curiosity of the young.

'That's right. Shopping. She took the bus. You were sleeping—'

'I miss Mommy.'

'So do I. But we'll see her soon enough.'

Daddy did some things with the dashboard and the wheel, and the car motor roared. Bobby liked that sound. It always meant going places and doing things. Though not very often with Daddy. Daddy was always away— packing bags, calling on the telephone from far-away places like Washington, DC, and hardly ever having time to play games or go walking in the woods. Bobby wasn't too sure what Daddy did—he didn't go to work like the fathers of his friends, or leave the house in the morning and come back the same day for supper, or play catch— no, nothing like that.

Bobby only knew that the big man's work had something to do with the shiny badge he had seen pinned inside the black wallet that was sometimes left on the bureau in the bedroom. That and that scary gun he sometimes saw when Daddy was putting on his jacket. He remembered he had once tried to pick it up, and his father had been very cross with him for it. Bobby knew he'd never to do *that* again!

Robert Black, Sr. patted his son affectionately on the cheek and released the emergency brake. Bobby knew what he was doing. The brake always made a funny sound when Daddy touched it with his hand.

'Now, Bobby—what is it you're going to remember?'

'Not to throw anything out of the car window.'

'Right. So if we stop for candy or gum, you'll fold up the wrappers neatly and give them to me, and I'll put them in the ashtray. OK?'

'OK.'

'You know last time when you tossed that paper bag out of the car window, it blew all the way back against the windshield of the car right behind us. The man couldn't see where he was going or what he was doing. He might have gotten hurt and you wouldn't want that, would you?'

'No, Daddy.'

'Good boy. Well, we're off.'

Daddy backed the Impala down the driveway. The line of trees looked so pretty in the sunlight. The big man turned the car around, heading it out towards the highway, his thick wrists relaxed, his large hands holding the wheel lightly. Bobby recognized the big school building with the American flag flying above it; next year he'd be going there like the rest of the kids.

He sank back happily against the soft seat and folded his arms. It was nice going someplace with Daddy for a change, instead of Mommy. Mommies were nice and fun, too, when they went to stores and places, but Daddies were better.

And Daddies never cried, while Mommies did. Like last night—

'Daddy, who was that man on the phone last night? The one who said something to make Mommy cry? Was it the man who got hit with the paper bag—did he want you to spank me?'

Robert Black, Sr. smiled, but it was a humourless smile, a grim smile.

'No, son. It was a bad man. It was a man who thought he could keep me from doing my job if he threatened—' Robert Black, Sr. suddenly closed his mouth. 'It was just a bad man, son. Forget it.'

'Why did Mommy cry?'

'I told you to forget it, Bobby. The man wasn't very nice. Like the big bad wolf in Red Riding Hood—'

'Or in the Three Little Pigs?'

'That's right. Don't worry. He won't call any more. Not after these papers are delivered in Elmira.'

Robert Black, Sr.'s mind was on the road and the traffic; Robert Black, Jr. was thinking of all the things he could tell Mommy that happened that morning after she left. About the loose front tooth, the striped kitten he had found wandering in the back yard, that nest of chirping sparrows in the carport.

And the wonderful breakfast of French toast with syrup that Daddy had made. Daddies could cook good, too, just like Mommies.

'Daddy?'

'Yes, son?'

'What's FBI mean?'

Robert Black, Sr. chuckled. 'Who told you that?'

'I was watching television with a couple of the other kids, and they said you were a FBI man. Are you, Daddy?'

'Billy and Gary, I imagine. The neighbourhood stool pigeons. What we need are about eight guys like them available to the Department. Well, they were telling you the truth, Bobby. I'm an FBI man.'

'What's that? Some kind of policeman?'

'That's right. It means the Federal Bureau of Investigation. That's my job. You knew I was some kind of a policeman, didn't you?'

'I guess so.'

The Impala zipped ahead, going around a flying big blue car. Daddy drove like a race-car driver. Bobby beamed proudly.

'Is Mommy glad you're a FBI man?'

Robert Black, Sr. shook his head, amused. 'Sometimes I wonder, son.'

'She gets—*afraid*? Like last night?'

'Sometimes. Women are like that, son. But it's a man's job, you know. And somebody has to do it.'

Bobby nodded his head wisely.

'I wouldn't be afraid. I'm proud you're a FBI man. Honest to Pete, I am.'

'Thanks, Bobby.'

Robert Black, Jr. glowed, glanced at his father, and was surprised to see the smile on the sharp features suddenly change to a frown. His mind searched for a reason for the obvious displeasure.

'What's the matter, Daddy? I didn't throw anything out of the window.'

His father's attention returned to the highway, a smile on his lips despite himself. 'No, but you did something almost as bad. You didn't fasten your seat belt. You always said you were big enough—'

'I *am* big enough!' Bobby's voice was stout.

He pulled the buckle from its place between his father and himself and then reached down between the seat and the door for the spring-retractable tongue that wound itself up into its holder when not in use, like that turtle Gary used to have, pulling its head in whenever you touched it.

His fingers found the end of the seat belt and he tugged it. It seemed to be stuck. He tugged harder without success and then leaned over, peering into the dim recess between the seat and the door.

A strange egg-shaped object was lying there where nothing had been before, apparently pulled from beneath the seat by his efforts, and now firmly wedged.

Bobby bent lower, working it loose, bringing it to his lap together with the end of the seat belt to which it was attached. He blinked at it, fascinated.

140

Robert Black, Sr., guiding the car along the highway at 60 miles an hour, wasn't looking anywhere but straight ahead. His profile was just like those policemen Bobby saw on television. Bobby sighed and returned his attention to the egg-shaped thing in his lap. He had never seen anything like it before.

It was made of metal and was heavy, and it had odd squarelike bumps all over it and a funny round pin in its top, held to the end of the seat belt by a thin strand of wire. He was sure Daddy would be interested, but first he had to obey his instructions. He tugged at the egg shape; it came away from the tongue of the seat belt, separating also from the little pin which now dangled comically. Bobby held the egg shape in his lap and latched the belt.

'Daddy—'

'Yes, son?' Robert Black, Sr. turned his head. And stared.

His face went white.

Bobby could never remember Daddy's eyes seeming so big or so *scary*. His face was all screwed up, like he had a toothache.

The roar of the car motor drowned out something that Daddy was yelling. There were so many other cars racing by, thundering, bulleting along the highway. Bobby whimpered in sudden fright.

His father's right arm shot out, flailing. Bobby recoiled, thinking for one awful second that Daddy was going to hit him.

He hugged the egg-shaped thing to his chest and shrank against the car door to make himself smaller.

Cars were hurtling forward, zooming ahead in a race for the sun and the horizon. A car horn blasted, frightening Bobby even more.

141

'Bobby!' Robert Black, Sr. screamed. 'Throw that thing out of the car!'

The flying trees, the ribbon of road, the thundering motors, and four vital seconds had fled.

'*Bobby!*'

'But, Daddy,' Robert Black, Jr. protested, his small face crumpled in confusion, 'you said never to—'

# On the Sidewalk, Bleeding

## EVAN HUNTER

The boy lay bleeding in the rain. He was sixteen years old, and he wore a bright purple silk jacket, and the lettering across the back of the jacket read THE ROYALS. The boy's name was Andy, and the name was delicately scripted in black thread on the front of the jacket, just over the heart. *Andy.*

He had been stabbed ten minutes ago. The knife had entered just below his rib cage and had been drawn across his body violently, tearing a wide gap in his flesh. He lay on the sidewalk with the March rain drilling his jacket and drilling his body and washing away the blood that poured from his open wound. He had known excruciating pain when the knife had torn across his body, and then sudden comparative relief when the blade was pulled away. He had heard the voice saying, 'That's for you, Royal!' and then the sound of footsteps hurrying into the rain, and then he had fallen to the sidewalk, clutching his stomach, trying to stop the flow of blood.

He tried to yell for help, but he had no voice. He did

not know why his voice had deserted him, or why the rain
had suddenly become so fierce, or why there was an open
hole in his body from which his life ran redly, steadily. It
was 11.30 p.m., but he did not know the time.

There was another thing he did not know.

He did not know he was dying. He lay on the sidewalk,
bleeding, and he thought only: *That was a fierce rumble.
They got me good that time*, but he did not know he was
dying. He would have been frightened had he known. In
his ignorance, he lay bleeding and wishing he could cry
out for help, but there was no voice in his throat. There
was only the bubbling of blood between his lips whenever
he opened his mouth to speak. He lay silent in his pain,
waiting, waiting for someone to find him.

He could hear the sound of automobile tyres hushed
on the muzzle of rainswept streets, far away at the other
end of the long alley. He lay with his face pressed to the
sidewalk, and he could see the splash of neon far away at
the other end of the alley, tinting the pavement red and
green, slickly brilliant in the rain.

He wondered if Laura would be angry.

He had left the jump to get a package of cigarettes. He
had told her he would be back in a few minutes, and then
he had gone downstairs and found the candy store closed.
He knew that Alfredo's on the next block would be open
until at least two, and he had started through the alley,
and that was when he'd been ambushed. He could hear
the faint sound of music now, coming from a long, long
way off, and he wondered if Laura was dancing, wondered
if she had missed him yet. Maybe she thought he wasn't
coming back. Maybe she thought he'd cut out for good.
Maybe she'd already left the jump and gone home.

He thought of her face, the brown eyes and the jet-black

hair, and thinking of her he forgot his pain a little, forgot that blood was rushing from his body. Someday he would marry Laura. Someday he would marry her, and they would have a lot of kids, and then they would get out of the neighbourhood. They would move to a clean project in the Bronx, or maybe they would move to Staten Island. When they were married, when they had kids . . .

He heard footsteps at the other end of the alley, and he lifted his cheek from the sidewalk and looked into the darkness and tried to cry out, but again there was only a soft hissing bubble of blood on his mouth.

The man came down the alley. He had not seen Andy yet. He walked, and then stopped to lean against the brick of the building, and then walked again. He saw Andy then and came towards him, and he stood over him for a long time, the minutes ticking, ticking, watching him and not speaking.

Then he said, 'What's a matter, buddy?'

Andy could not speak, and he could barely move. He lifted his face slightly and looked up at the man, and in the rainswept alley he smelled the sickening odour of alcohol and realized the man was drunk. He did not feel any particular panic. He did not know he was dying, and so he felt only mild disappointment that the man who had found him was drunk.

The man was smiling.

'Did you fall down, buddy?' he asked. 'You mus' be as drunk as I am.' He grinned, seemed to remember why he had entered the alley in the first place, and said, 'Don' go way. I'll be ri' back.'

The man lurched away. Andy heard his footsteps, and then the sound of the man colliding with a garbage can, and some mild swearing, and then the sound of the man urinating, lost in the steady wash of the rain. He waited for the man to come back.

It was 11.39.

When the man returned, he squatted alongside Andy. He studied him with drunken dignity.

'You gonna catch cold here,' he said. 'What's a matter? You like layin' in the wet?'

Andy could not answer. The man tried to focus his eyes on Andy's face. The rain spattered around them.

'You like a drink?'

Andy shook his head.

'I gotta bottle. Here,' the man said. He pulled a pint bottle from his inside jacket pocket. He uncapped it and extended it to Andy. Andy tried to move, but pain wrenched him back flat against the sidewalk.

'Take it,' the man said. He kept watching Andy. 'Take it.' When Andy did not move, he said, 'Nev' mind. I'll have one m'self.' He tilted the bottle to his lips, and then wiped the back of his hand across his mouth. 'You too young to be drinkin', anyway. Should be 'shamed of yourself, drunk an' laying in a alley, all wet. Shame on you. I gotta good minda calla cop.'

Andy nodded. Yes, he tried to say. Yes, call a cop. Please. Call one.

'Oh, you don' like that, huh?' the drunk said. 'You don' wanna cop to fin' you all drunk an' wet in a alley, huh? OK, buddy. This time you get off easy.' He got to his feet. 'This time you lucky,' he said. He waved broadly at Andy, and then almost lost his footing. 'S'long, buddy,' he said.

*Wait*, Andy thought. *Wait, please, I'm bleeding.*

'S'long,' the drunk said again. 'I see you aroun',' and then he staggered off up the alley.

146

Andy lay and thought: *Laura, Laura. Are you dancing?*

The couple came into the alley suddenly. They ran into the alley together, running from the rain, the boy holding the girl's elbow, the girl spreading a newspaper over her head to protect her hair. Andy lay crumpled against the pavement, and he watched them run into the alley laughing, and then duck into the doorway not ten feet from him.

'Man, what rain!' the boy said. 'You could drown out there.'

'I have to get home,' the girl said. 'It's late, Freddie. I have to get home.'

'We got time,' Freddie said. 'Your people won't raise a fuss if you're a little late. Not with this kind of weather.'

'It's dark,' the girl said, and she giggled.

'Yeah,' the boy answered, his voice very low.

'Freddie . . . ?'

'Um?'

'You're . . . you're standing very close to me.'

'Um.'

There was a long silence. Then the girl said, 'Oh,' only that single word, and Andy knew she'd been kissed, and he suddenly hungered for Laura's mouth. It was then that he wondered if he would ever kiss Laura again. It was then that he wondered if he was dying.

*No*, he thought, *I can't be dying, not from a little street rumble, not from just getting cut. Guys get cut all the time in rumbles. I can't be dying. No, that's stupid. That don't make any sense at all.*

'You shouldn't,' the girl said.

'Why not?'

'I don't know.'

147

'Do you like it?'

'Yes.'

'So?'

'I don't know.'

'I love you, Angela,' the boy said.

'I love you, too, Freddie,' the girl said, and Andy listened and thought: *I love you, Laura. Laura, I think maybe I'm dying. Laura, this is stupid but I think maybe I'm dying. Laura, I think I'm dying!*

He tried to speak. He tried to move. He tried to crawl towards the doorway where he could see the two figures in embrace. He tried to make a noise, a sound, and a grunt came from his lips, and then he tried again, and another grunt came, a low animal grunt of pain.

'What was that?' the girl said, suddenly alarmed, breaking away from the boy.

'I don't know,' he answered.

'Go look, Freddie.'

'No. Wait.'

Andy moved his lips again. Again the sound came from him.

'Freddie!'

'What?'

'I'm scared.'

'I'll go see,' the boy said.

He stepped into the alley. He walked over to where Andy lay on the ground. He stood over him, watching him.

'You all right?' he asked.

'What is it?' Angela said from the doorway.

'Somebody's hurt,' Freddie said.

'Let's get out of here,' Angela said.

'No. Wait a minute.' He knelt down beside Andy. 'You cut?' he asked.

Andy nodded. The boy kept looking at him. He saw the lettering on the jacket then. THE ROYALS. He turned to Angela.

'He's a Royal,' he said.

'Let's . . . what . . . what do you want to do, Freddie?'

'I don't know. I don't want to get mixed up in this. He's a Royal. We help him, and the Guardians'll be down on our necks. I don't want to get mixed up in this, Angela.'

'Is he . . . is he hurt bad?'

'Yeah, it looks that way.'

'What shall we do?'

'I don't know.'

'We can't leave him here in the rain.' Angela hesitated. 'Can we?'

'If we get a cop, the Guardians'll find out who,' Freddie said. 'I don't know, Angela. I don't know.'

Angela hesitated a long time before answering. Then she said, 'I have to get home, Freddie. My people will begin to worry.'

'Yeah,' Freddie said. He looked at Andy again. 'You all right?' he asked. Andy lifted his face from the sidewalk, and his eyes said: *Please, please help me*, and maybe Freddie read what his eyes were saying, and maybe he didn't.

Behind him, Angela said, 'Freddie, let's get out of here! Please!' There was urgency in her voice, urgency bordering on the edge of panic. Freddie stood up. He looked at Andy again, and then mumbled, 'I'm sorry,' and then he took Angela's arm and together they ran towards the neon splash at the other end of the alley.

*Why, they're afraid of the Guardians*, Andy thought in

amazement. *But why should they be? I wasn't afraid of the Guardians. I never turkeyed out of a rumble with the Guardians. I got heart. But I'm bleeding.*

The rain was soothing somehow. It was a cold rain, but his body was hot all over, and the rain helped to cool him. He had always liked rain. He could remember sitting in Laura's house one time, the rain running down the windows, and just looking out over the street, watching the people running from the rain. That was when he'd first joined the Royals. He could remember how happy he was the Royals had taken him. The Royals and the Guardians, two of the biggest. He was a Royal. There had been meaning to the title.

Now, in the alley, with the cold rain washing his hot body, he wondered about the meaning. If he died, he was Andy. He was not a Royal. He was simply Andy, and he was dead. And he wondered suddenly if the Guardians who had ambushed him and knifed him had ever once realized he was Andy? Had they known that he was Andy, or had they simply known that he was a Royal wearing a purple silk jacket? Had they stabbed *him*, Andy, or had they only stabbed the jacket and the title, and what good was the title if you were dying?

*I'm Andy*, he screamed wordlessly. *For Christ's sake. I'm Andy!*

An old lady stopped at the other end of the alley. The garbage cans were stacked there, beating noisily in the rain. The old lady carried an umbrella with broken ribs, carried it with all the dignity of a queen. She stepped into the mouth of the alley, a shopping bag over one arm. She lifted the lids of the garbage cans delicately, and she did not hear Andy grunt because she was a little deaf and because the rain was beating a steady relentless tattoo on the cans. She had been searching and foraging for the better part of the night. She collected her string and her newspapers, and an old hat with a feather on it from one of the garbage cans, and a broken footstool from another of the cans. And then she delicately replaced the lids and lifted her umbrella high and walked out of the alley mouth with queenly dignity. She had worked swiftly and soundlessly, and now she was gone.

The alley looked very long now. He could see people passing at the other end of it, and he wondered who the people were, and he wondered if he would ever get to know them, wondered who it was on the Guardians who had stabbed him, who had plunged the knife into his body.

'That's for you, Royal!' the voice had said, and then the footsteps, his arms being released by the others, the fall to the pavement. 'That's for you, Royal!' Even in his pain, even as he collapsed, there had been some sort of pride in knowing he was a Royal. Now there was no pride at all. With the rain beginning to chill him, with the blood pouring steadily between his fingers, he knew only a sort of dizziness, and within the giddy dizziness, he could only think: *I want to be Andy.*

It was not very much to ask of the world.

He watched the world passing at the other end of the alley. The world didn't know he was Andy. The world didn't know he was alive. He wanted to say, 'Hey, I'm alive! Hey, look at me! I'm alive! Don't you know I'm alive? Don't you know I exist?'

He felt weak and very tired. He felt alone and wet and feverish and chilled, and he knew he was going to die now, and the knowledge made him suddenly sad. He was not frightened. For some reason, he was not frightened.

He was only filled with an overwhelming sadness that his life would be over at sixteen. He felt all at once as if he had never done anything, never seen anything, never been anywhere. There were so many things to do, and he wondered why he'd never thought of them before, wondered why the rumbles and the jumps and the purple jacket had always seemed so important to him before, and now they seemed like such small things in a world he was missing, a world that was rushing past at the other end of the alley.

*I don't want to die*, he thought. *I haven't lived yet.*

It seemed very important to him that he take off the purple jacket. He was very close to dying, and when they found him, he did not want them to say, 'Oh, it's a Royal.' With great effort, he rolled over on to his back. He felt the pain tearing at his stomach when he moved, a pain he did not think was possible. But he wanted to take off the jacket. If he never did another thing, he wanted to take off the jacket. The jacket had only one meaning now, and that was a very simple meaning.

If he had not been wearing the jacket, he would not have been stabbed. The knife had not been plunged in hatred of Andy. The knife hated only the purple jacket. The jacket was a stupid meaningless thing that was robbing him of his life. He wanted the jacket off his back. With an enormous loathing, he wanted the jacket off his back.

He lay struggling with the shiny wet material. His arms were heavy, and pain ripped fire across his body whenever he moved. But he squirmed and fought and twisted until one arm was free and then the other, and then he rolled away from the jacket and lay quite still, breathing heavily, listening to the sound of his breathing and the sound of the rain and thinking: *Rain is sweet, I'm Andy.*

She found him in the alleyway a minute past midnight. She left the dance to look for him, and when she found him she knelt beside him and said, 'Andy, it's me, Laura.'

He did not answer her. She backed away from him, tears springing into her eyes, and then she ran from the alley hysterically and did not stop running until she found the cop.

And now, standing with the cop, she looked down at him, and the cop rose and said, 'He's dead,' and all the crying was out of her now. She stood in the rain and said nothing, looking at the dead boy on the pavement, and looking at the purple jacket that rested a foot away from his body.

The cop picked up the jacket and turned it over in his hands.

'A Royal, huh?' he said.

The rain seemed to beat more steadily now, more fiercely.

She looked at the cop and, very quietly, she said, 'His name is Andy.'

The cop slung the jacket over his arm. He took out his black pad, and he flipped it open to a blank page.

'A Royal,' he said.

Then he began writing.

# Acknowledgements

**Marc Alexander:** 'Sweet Shop', reprinted from *Not After Nightfall* (Kestrel, 1985), copyright © Marc Alexander 1985, by arrangement with Rupert Crew Limited.

**Michael Avallone:** 'Every Litter Bit Hurts', copyright © 1968 by Michael Avallone, first published in *Ellery Queen's Mystery Magazine*, 1968. Copyright holder not traced.

**Robert Barr:** 'An Alpine Divorce', taken from Hugh Lamb (ed.): *Stories in the Dark*, Equation Chillers 1989, but first published in Robert Barr: *Revenge!* Chatto & Windus 1896.

**Ambrose Bierce:** 'The Middle Toe of the Right Foot', from *Can Such Things Be?*

**Sydney J. Bounds:** 'Ghost Hunter', copyright © Sydney J. Bounds 1981, first published in Mary Danby (ed.): *The 13th Armada Ghost Book* (Fontana, 1981), reprinted by permission of the author.

**Ray Bradbury:** 'The Veldt', reprinted from *The Illustrated Man* (Rupert Hart-Davis, 1952), copyright © 1950 by the Curtis Publishing Co., renewed 1977 by Ray Bradbury, by permission of Don Congdon Associates, Inc.

**Fredric Brown:** 'Voodoo', copyright © 1954 by Galaxy Publishing Association, copyright renewed by Fredric Brown, reprinted by permission of A. M. Heath & Co. Ltd and the Scott Meredith Literary Agency on behalf of the Late Fredric Brown.

**Ethel Helene Coen:** 'One Chance', first published in *Weird Tales* magazine, reprinted by permission of Victor Dricks/Weird Tales Ltd.

**John Collier:** 'Thus I Refute Beelzy', reprinted from *The John Collier Reader* (Souvenir Press, 1975), copyright © 1951 by John Collier, renewed 1979 by the Estate of John Collier, by permission of Harold Matson Co., Inc.

**Roald Dahl:** 'The Landlady', reprinted from *Kiss Kiss* (Michael Joseph, 1960), by permission of David Higham Associates.

**Richard and Judy Dockrey Young:** 'The Skeleton in the Closet', reprinted from *The Scary Story Reader* by Richard and Judy Dockrey Young (August House, 1993), copyright © 1993 by Richard and Judy Dockrey Young, by permission of August House Publishers, Inc., c/o Marian Reiner.